TILL THE OTHER SIDE OF TIME

Disclaimer: This book is the second part of a series. You will need to read *Tell Me You Want Me* by Kris Embrey to understand the story line of this book in its entirety.

TILL THE OTHER SIDE OF TIME

Kris Embrey

ARCHWAY
PUBLISHING

Archway Publishing
1663 Liberty Drive
Bloomington, IN 47403
www.archwaypublishing.com
1 (888) 242-5904

Cover illustration designed by Lane Bullard.

ISBN: 978-1-4808-4729-3 (sc)
ISBN: 978-1-4808-4730-9 (hc)
ISBN: 978-1-4808-4731-6 (e)

Library of Congress Control Number: 2017909117

Print information available on the last page.

Archway Publishing rev. date: 08/21/2017

To Sally, my best friend through a lifetime.
To Wayne. I got a pair of Jacks. Are we there yet?
To Lane. Time flies when you're manic.
To Mark T. and Ron. You were both right … I'm not right.
To Zoltan. I'm selling books in Budapest?
To Ahou. "Rubies, darling. Rubies."
To Tina. Namaste, bitches.
To Julio, "Prince." (That's it … Prince.)
To Raul. So, I have this problem with my
computer … wine club, flight club.
To Laura. It's been a journey.
To Beth. Thanks, friend.
To the meaningful coincidence.

Synchronicity

A wild mustang is hard to tame,
a bird in flight, easily the same.
Like a desert that calls to the sun,
my heart knew you were the one.
Synchronicity opened the door,
always had me wanting more.
Songs and signs that came every day,
dimes in my path, left along the way.
A rainbow's end came early in May,
no reason to believe you'd fly away.
Excuses became abundant, that much is true,
they can't hold me, and they don't hold you.
See you again? Sure, maybe one day.
Synchronicity before we met,
you mentioned it, by the way.
So, pick up the dime that was meant for me.
It's synchronicity at work; funny how the universe can be.
Keep that smile you have, and always stay true.
Someday you might think of me;
synchronicity won't let me forget about you.

—Kris Embrey

The Book of Leon

NBC Studios, New York, August 12, 1988
Leon Taylor interview, already in progress.

> *Interviewer*: You were on the infamous 'Wait (Wait
> till I'm Home) Tour.' Is that correct?

> *Leon*: Yes, I was.

> *Interviewer*: It was rumored that the tour was plagued
> with drug problems.

> *Leon*: (laughing) I never heard that rumor.

> *Interviewer*: Sebastian Roland has a reputation with
> issues related to drugs like heroin. Can
> you comment on that?

> *Leon*: Heroin? No, I've never seen him or anyone do
> smack … okay?

I should've had the sense to decline the interview. I wasn't expecting to be asked about drug use during a tour that happened over two years ago. I disconnected from the interviewer when I got hit with that last ignorant-ass question, which caused my mind to go back to that crazy tour and what followed after Gina and I left it.

It was November 17, 1986, when I started unpacking from the move into Gina's and my new apartment. I had just pulled the last of the kitchen nonsense out from a box when the phone rang.

"Leon, hey, it's Walter. Listen to this … you'll never believe who I just got off the phone with," he said with excitement.

"Who?" I asked, preoccupied.

"Guess who's still lighting matches to Gina torch?" Walter said, laughing.

"Are you serious?" I replied, surprised. I knew who Walter was referring to and started whispering over the phone because Gina was sitting on the other side of the room.

"Sebastian tried calling you at your old number. He told me he'd made a big mistake. Can you believe that?" Walter said.

"He's a damn mess," I replied, rolling my eyes.

Walter proceeded to enlighten me on his conversation with Sebastian. I knew that man had called Bridgette's place several times looking for Gina only because B had been bitching to me nonstop about it. Sebastian probably assumed that if he called the Christopher apartment enough times, Gina would answer the phone. Bridgette had finally had enough and had told Sebastian in a more animated way to go kick rocks and stop calling. Sebastian must have finally given up on Bridgette and figured that, since he used to hit Walter up for drugs back in the day, they were tight enough for Walter to give him info about where Gina was staying now. Walter didn't give Sebastian the information he was digging for; instead, Walter called me and asked, "What do you want to do about it?" Thinking about his question and looking over at Gina, who was staring off into space and looking out the window, I told Walter to give me Sebastian's number. I'm the one who decided to make the call to Sebastian.

I was really mad at Sebastian for what he'd done to Gina at that video shoot, not to mention the other things I had heard about on tour that had been kept from Gina. It was fair to say that Sebastian auditioned his tool in anything that had an opening, if you get my meaning. He was a damn mess with it. I'm being real with you. I didn't want to be part of their love shit; it was exhausting. But she was hurting and still in love with his dumb ass, so I had to do something.

Gina had put on her coat and was heading over to Bridgette's for the day. "See you later," she said somberly. I was still on the phone with Walter.

After she left, I picked up the phone and placed the call to Sebastian. I will admit, I was curious myself about what had happened with him after the tour ended. Looking at his number, which I had scribbled on the side of a moving box, I thought about what I was going to say to his ass. I dialed the operator to place a London call, collect of course.

"This is the United States operator. Collect call from the makeup lady to Mr. SoBo Roland. Will you accept the charges?" the operator said when Sebastian answered.

"Makeup lady? Leon? Yeah, I'll accept," Sebastian answered back.

"Go ahead makeup lady," the operator answered back.

"Hello, Sebastian" I said after some hesitation when he was switched over. He seemed a bit surprised to hear my voice on the other end.

"Where is she, Leon?" Sebastian asked impatiently, and he spent the first few minutes of our conversation pushing on me how to reach Gina and droning on about how he missed her.

"She's around … busy, but she's around," I replied, ignoring his tale of woe. I glanced out the window to see that heavy snow had started falling. I was personally anticipating some warmer weather in Europe, so as I watched the snow, I began thinking about whether I should pack a speedo to take to Greece.

"I fucked up, Leon. I'm coming to New York for Christmas to see her," he said.

He was still going on about how sorry he was for what he did to Gina when, without thinking, I let the cat out of the bag, interrupting to let him know that Gina and I were headed to Greece for Christmas.

"Really?" Sebastian said. He paused and then started to regale me with some foolishness about how he was going to meet us there and ask Gina to marry him. I thought he was crazy until he said, "Keep it a secret from her."

This fucking man. I had to keep that info tight for three weeks. He wanted me to get Gina to the Acropolis the day we landed. He knew she'd always wanted to go there, so that was where he was going to ask her to marry his dumb ass, but he needed my help.

After I hung up with Sebastian, I called Walter back and told him about our little conversation and Sebastian's plan to meet us in Greece.

"That's romantic," he said.

Of course he would think some mess like that, because he was living a straight life now. Walter was a yester-gay (yesterday gay) with a baby on the way. I rolled my eyes. Walter didn't have to live with

Gina or Sebastian's secret. I did. I was edged off at Walter for getting me involved in this foolishness.

After Gina and I had landed in Athens, we checked into our very posh hotel. I, being very eager to get this Sebastian thing out of the way, said that I wanted to see the Acropolis. Gina wanted to sit on the balcony with some cocktails looking at it from a distance and go there the following day. After a half hour of sitting on the balcony and a few Manhattans, I finally talked her into going. I wasn't taking no for an answer. It could be difficult to get Gina to do things she didn't want to do except on her timeline, but she always gave in to me because we were tight like that.

I proceeded to get her together and proposal-ready for the day, and when she asked why, I said, "Girl, sit. Let me have my moment. Don't be so damn difficult." We finally left the hotel for the Acropolis. I'll admit I was somewhat anxious about this meeting going down on her like that. I wanted to tell her that Sebastian had called and tell her what he was going to do, but I decided that this was their day, not mine.

I looked at my watch as we headed over. I had about twenty minutes before I had to meet up with Sebastian. We got our admission tickets, and Gina and I started up the stairs. She wanted to find the Parthenon and then sit by herself and have me meet her there later. I knew she wanted to sit and have a pity party for one, and her desire to be by herself made it really easy for me to deal with Sebastian alone. Crying over his dumb ass, girl ... really?

When we found the Parthenon, Gina said she needed thirty minutes, and I beat heels out of there to meet Sebastian near the front entrance. As I stood there looking around, I glanced at my watch and noticed he was a few minutes late. I thought, *If he doesn't show up, do I tell Gina about this? It has been three weeks; he might have changed his mind.* He was ten minutes late, and I was ready to give up on him and go get Gina. When I turned around, I heard Sebastian yell, "Leon!" He was moving fast to approach me.

"Hey, Leon," Sebastian said as I waited until he approached.

"Sorry, I tore ass to get here," Sebastian said, a bit nervous.

"How are you, Sebastian?" I said, disinterested in his answer.

"Good. Where's Gina?" he replied, looking around for her.

"Sitting on a bunch of old rocks," I replied.

As we started our walk up the stairs to the area where Gina was, he was asking me nervous questions like, what had I been up to since the tour? He wanted to know what she had been doing since she'd left it so abruptly. I wasn't going to say, "Crying over your dumb ass every day." Instead I told him she was great and doing very well. Figured I'd keep him guessing. We got to the edge of the steps, and I pointed over to where she was sitting. Sebastian was looking at her from a distance and kept saying to himself, "I'm so sorry, baby," but he didn't move. He just stood there.

"Stop the shit, Sebastian. Go and get her," I told him. He pissed me off.

Sebastian snapped out of his stare down and had started walking with fierce determination when Gina stood up. I tailed behind his ass. I wanted to see and hear everything. I mean, I got her there and knew what was getting ready to go down. I wasn't going to miss this shit for anything. He slowed down when he got about five feet behind her. I stood back from him until they made contact. He was surveying her every move.

"Tell me you forgive me," Sebastian said as Gina was looking out over Athens.

Gina heard his voice and slowly turned around. She had tears in her eyes. "Oh my God ... Sebastian?" she said, startled and in disbelief,

"How are you, G?" Sebastian asked her, chill-like.

"What are you doing here?" Gina asked, confused and in shock—rightfully so.

"I messed up, G. Really bad." Sebastian replied.

Yeah, you did, I thought.

"I came all the way to Greece to see you," he said, taking her hand.

"You came to Greece to see me?" she asked, confused.

"Well, I wanted to ask you a question." He held onto her hand as he got down on one knee and pulled out of his pocket the biggest damn ring I had ever seen. "Will you marry me, Gina Kelly?" Sebastian asked her, holding the ring up to her and waiting for her answer.

"You can skate on that ice!" I said. Sebastian and Gina looked over at me like I was crazy. "Oh, I'm sorry. I didn't mean to take over your moment, but I've known this was coming for three weeks. So, go on." I wanted to get this over and get back to the bar.

"I can't, Sebastian," Gina said, pulling her hand away from him then walking away in a huff.

I stood there looking at Sebastian. I was confused as hell and thought she was crazy. I mean, Gina had been trippin' out over this man for more than a few months. I was thinking, *Girl, what? Please, say something positive to his stupid ass and leave me the fuck alone with this.*

Sebastian was still on one knee, looking at me confused. He stood up and took off after her with me following behind him again.

"Gina, I've been in a treatment program since the tour ended. I've been sober for a month. Gina, I give you my word. I'm clean," Sebastian said, as she continued walking.

"No, Sebastian, you wasted your time coming here," Gina said, never turning around and walking further away.

"Gina, please don't walk away," Sebastian said, very confused.

I was thinking, *Damn, girl, you must be crazy. You have been crying over this man's nasty ass for two months.*

"Gina, please let me explain," Sebastian said, pleading with her.

Gina stopped and turned around. "Sebastian, you really have nerve coming here after you broke my heart. Hooking up with your ex-girlfriend … in front of me? It was you who set the tone for this relationship, not me. You're an asshole, Sebastian," she said like a real OG. I wanted to applaud her, actually.

The three of us were standing there, and Sebastian was looking at me like I had done something to set her off. Tourists were passing by us, trying to observe what was going on without looking obvious. I was trying to keep a straight face when I shrugged my shoulders and told him, "I really thought she would say yes. She is trippin', though."

The three of us squared off, standing in a triangle formation and looking at each other, waiting to see who was going to say something next. Sebastian said that he had never dated the girl from the video shoot, which Gina and I both knew was bullshit. I mean, he had slept with that girl more than a few times in the past. Gina folded her arms and gave him a look that said, "You are crazy with that story."

"Okay, Gina … I was never in love with her. I was pissed off at you. I didn't think you'd actually leave the tour," he said, frustrated, finally telling her the truth.

"Sebastian, you really are a piece of work. The amount of crap you put me through caused enough hurt to last anyone a lifetime. It's your loss, Sebastian. Sorry things didn't work out the way you wanted with your video slut," Gina said before walking away.

"I love you, Gina. I know I fucked us up," Sebastian yelled out to her with tears in his eyes.

This was getting serious. He started crying and looking over at me. It made me feel sorry for his ass, really, because the whole proposal thing had backfired on him.

"I'm sorry I hurt you," Sebastian said pleadingly.

Gina turned around and gave him a nasty look. "Lacey must have told you that Tiger's looking for me … Goodbye, Sebastian." She walked away from us in a huff.

It was pretty cold of her to say that to him, actually, and it embarrassed the hell out of me for them both, because what she said wasn't true.

"Gina! … You really know how to cut someone and make them bleed. Don't do this to us," Sebastian yelled out to her.

"Sebastian, there is no more us. That story ended in DC when you broke my heart," she snapped back before walking away.

Sebastian looked down at the ring he'd bought for her. The sun was hitting it just right, and the only thing that was sparkling was that five-carat diamond he had in his hand. I wondered how much that had set him back. I felt sorry for him. I put my hand on his back and asked him to wait while I went and talked to her. Hell, I was as confused by her rejection of him as he was.

I caught up to Gina and asked, "What's up?" Gina snapped back at me for telling Sebastian we were in Greece. As Gina and I were having our argument about me setting this up, I saw Sebastian walk toward us. And the rest? Well, this mess really is history.

"Damn it, G ... I fucked up!" Sebastian said angrily with tears in his eyes.

"Yeah, you did, but more than once, Sebastian," she said, looking at him seriously.

"You're the one, Gina," Sebastian said, with a defeated look on his face. He wiped away his tears, never breaking eye contact with her. "Say yes."

Gina looked at him and hesitated for a few seconds. Something inside her clicked; I saw it in her eyes as she tilted her head. She looked at him with a half-hearted smile and told him that if he stayed clean and sober for at least six months, she would consider marrying his stupid ass. Sebastian went and put his arms around her. They held each other and said nothing after that. After a few seconds, Sebastian broke his embrace, took Gina by the hand, and lead her away.

I laughed to myself as they got further from my sight. "You all are a hot damn mess."

I have seen some shit in my life but never two people who did crazier shit to each other than these two did. Gina and Sebastian's relationship could be tumultuous at times, but they found their way back to one another. They were connected in some strange way that I will never understand, and you could feel it being around them.

I headed back to the hotel after they left. I wanted to hit Walter up with the play-by-play of this mess. It was classic G and Bas drama, and in this circle, you dial a friend, girl.

After I replayed the proposal drama for Walter, I headed downstairs to the hotel bar. A few hours had passed, and I was a little liquored up by the time these two love birds came in laughing and kissing on each other. Gina was holding a bag from a jewelry store.

"Now this is a Kodak moment. Oh ... Bridgette is going to be so pissed when she sees this shit," I said, laughing at them. I ordered another drink. I had come to Greece to dry out, but I was currently on my way to a full sail. Sebastian leaned against the bar and ordered a soda pop, which confused the hell out of me. I'd always seen him with a beer bottle in one hand and Gina's ass in the other.

Gina was smiling. She frantically pulled a box out from the bag she was holding. I was taking a sip of my cocktail when Sebastian announced that he and Gina were going to have a very impromptu wedding in Greece. She shoved something in my face. Starring at the black-diamond wedding band she had bought for his dumb ass, I choked on my drink. I got straight a minute, well enough to get off my bar stool and pull her to the side to talk some sense into her.

"You really need to rethink this shit, Gina. You told him six months, girl." At that moment, all I could think about was that Bridgette would have my ass when she heard about this craziness.

I sat back down on my bar stool, looking at Sebastian like he lost his damn mind. He told how they wanted to just go ahead and do it "the day before you head to Italy." I deduced from the *you* in that proclamation that Gina wouldn't be making it to Milan with me for Christmas. Yep, Bridgette was going have my ass.

Sebastian said he needed to make some phone calls, and I closed out my bar tab. The three of us left the bar and started our walk back to our room, which began to sober me up. As we got off the elevator, those two were giggling. I opened the door and went to lay down, as my head was all twisted up. Sebastian walked over to a chair near the phone and said he needed to place a call to his parents, probably to ask for help with the embassy and all the red tape they needed to get through for this half-assed wedding.

"Dad, I need you and *Mitera* to come to Athens for a family emergency," he said. He then talked with them for a few minutes before hanging up and calling Rick.

I was still in shock from the news when Gina announced she was calling Bridgette. I held on to my pillow, imagining Bridgette yelling at me, and tried to tell her it wasn't a great idea to be calling B with this marriage news right now. I knew that if Gina did, B would jump on the next flight and then jump on my ass. I lay there looking at them both, drunk as fuck, wondering why in the hell I'd gotten involved in this.

The Book of Bridgette

Imagine my reaction when I got a phone call from Gina the day she landed in Greece.

"Bridgette, can you come to Athens? … I just got engaged," Gina said, fighting back tears.

"What? Gina, are you serious with this right now?" I said, angered.

"I'm getting married the day after tomorrow in Athens. I want you to be here, because you're like a sister to me and I love you," Gina said with hesitation in her voice.

"Who are you marrying, Gina?" I asked her, knowing the answer.

After a long pause on the other end of the phone, she sheepishly replied, "Sebastian."

"*Fottermi!*" I said, slamming the phone down on her. I worked out that Leon must have been involved in this reunion somehow. All I could think was, *This man broke your heart, and now he has come back to you with some bullshit about getting married?* She called me back.

"Why did you hang up on me, Bridgette? I know you don't like him, but I love him. I want you to be a little happy for me. Can you please be here tomorrow?" Gina asked, whining.

"Gina, I hope you know what you're doing," I said, aggravated. I knew Gina needed me, and of course I was going to be there for her. I didn't agree with her decision, but I did need to support my best friend. She was like a sister to me.

After I hung up the phone, I went to my room and threw some things in my bag. I told my parents I would be back in a few days and headed to the airport, where I took the last available seat on the two-hour flight to Athens. I did all of this, including flying to Greece, in less than three hours. On the flight, I was stewing in my seat and getting increasingly pissed off at Leon for not telling me about any of this bullshit before he and Gina left New York. I knew Leon had set this up. Sebastian had been calling me for weeks looking for Gina. I already knew what had happened. Leon had been seduced by the Louis Vuitton–purchasing lunatic.

By the time I landed and got into a cab, I was even more aggravated. I headed to the Hotel Grande Bretagne, where Leon and Gina were staying. They weren't expecting me until the next day.

When I got to the hotel and checked in, I demanded Gina and Leon's room number from the front desk. I told them my sister was being manipulated by a deranged maniac and that I was here to pay her a surprise visit.

I arrived at room 515 and actually pounded on their door with my fist in aggravation. I could hear Leon in the room.

"Shit, room service be knocking like they the damn police," he said. He opened the door, saw my face, and then shut it again. I could hear him screaming like a little girl on the other side.

"Open up this door, Leon," I yelled. There was commotion in the room, and Gina came to the door. "Where the fuck is he?" I said, barging in, looking for Leon.

"He's in the bathroom, Bridgette. Be nice," Gina said as she grabbed my arm, pleading with me to leave Leon be.

"Leon, come out of the bathroom," I demanded, pounding on the door and ignoring her.

"No way. You're going to kick my ass. Probably brought the damn mafia with you too, girl. Fuck that," Leon said, acting like a spoiled child.

"Leon, come out of the bathroom. This is stupid," I said.

Leon cracked opened the door, and I pushed it open on him and went in.

"You have some fucking nerve keeping this from me," I yelled, slapping him on the back of the head.

"Ouch. Damn, that hurt, bitch," Leon said, putting his hand to the back of his head. He got scared when I went after him, and he ran out of the bathroom. "If I end up dead, you know this bitch made a phone call to her friends, Gina!" He was screaming and jumped on the bed as I approached him.

"Stop it! Bridgette, stop it now," Gina demanded. As I backed off of Leon, she put her arms around me, showing me her extravagant engagement ring. Leon jumped off the bed and went near Sebastian for protection. I gave Sebastian the stare-down as he sat there in that chair, but he wasn't paying attention to any of the commotion. His

Royal Highness was on the phone speaking Greek. Typical Sebastian, flippant and unresponsive.

Sebastian and Gina part two was not something I wanted to be involved in, but I needed to be. We'd all picked up the pieces after she left the tour, and I was over this wedding before it even started.

The Book of Gina

My wedding to Sebastian was the happiest moment of my life. I was marrying the love of my life in a place I had always wanted to come to. I called my parents, and of course they were happy for me. But on the phone, my dad told me that Sebastian had already asked permission for my hand in marriage. Sebastian had asked Leon for my parent's number before we left for Greece. They were pleased that he'd called to ask but couldn't make it for the wedding.

Bridgette had left our room to go change into something more suitable for the afternoon, and Sebastian was getting ready to run some errands.

"Babe, I know this is going to sound really odd coming from me, but … I want to wait to be with you until we say our I-do's." He gave me a hug. "I'll call you later. I still want to hear your voice before I go to bed."

This left me with a feeling of butterflies in my stomach. He was sober, and he was different. He was relaxed and kind.

He went over to Leon. "Take care of my girl," he said, before leaving our room.

Leon and I were left alone, and with a stern look, he said, "I can't believe you're not going to wait and see if he is off the shit before you marry his ass. I'm gonna call Lacey and see what's been going on with him." Leon went riffling through his suitcase, throwing things on the floor, digging for his address book. Pulling out a black book with very worn pages, he placed a person-to-person call to Lacey. He sat on hold, waiting for an operator. It was late in the states. I suggested he wait until the morning, but Leon insisted to leave him be.

He settled down on his bed, crossing his legs and waiting patiently to be connected. He gave me a pensive look as he said, "Lacey, it's Leon girl. What's up? … Oh, nothing. Hey, girl, I wanted to ask you a question. What's been going on with SoBo? Is he still fucking that video girl and using the shit?"

As Leon was speaking to Lacey on the phone, there was a knock at the door. Bridgette had come back, dressed and ready to hit the town. I went into the hall so she wouldn't hear what Leon was saying, telling her he was on the phone and that I wanted to give him some privacy. I went back into the room and motioned to Leon that we were going to the bar. He gave me an eye roll and a dismissive hand gesture that implied that we should go and he would meet us after his call.

Bridgette and I went to the bar and ordered drinks, getting caught up on each other's lives over the last few weeks. We were both happy to get a reprieve from the cold weather of Manhattan. Leon spotted us and walked toward us. He took a seat on the other side of me. "We'll talk later girl," was his comment in my ear.

As Leon ordered a drink, Bridgette got up and said she needed to use the ladies room. When Bridgette got out of Leon's line of sight, he turned to me. "Girl, according to Lacey, you're the reason Sebastian put his ass into rehab, and as far as the video girl? She was a slump-buster after his ex … they were never serious."

"Slumpbuster? What the hell is that?" I asked, confused,

"You ain't never heard of a booty call? Girl, don't even trip," Leon said dismissively.

Lacey was in the know with all things SoBo. She was well dialed in on all his antics. She had known him for years, and they were friends. Lacey had dated Sebastian's best friend Joe from Raider's on and off and was exposed to his more personal side. According to Leon's conversation with Lacey, Sebastian had dated the video girl after he and his wife broke up, but she said they were never serious. Sebastian evidently got a bad case of the four-week crazies while we were touring Europe, according to Lacey, and he told Stan to hire the girl for the video shoot just to piss me off. According to Lacey, Stan had told Sebastian that I would leave if he hired the girl, but he had Stan do it anyway, just to get a reaction out of me. Sebastian used this girl to get back at me for "something I did to him," according to Lacey. I assumed that it was not wanting to get pregnant on his timeline.

The idea of using people to hurt someone you are supposed to love really made my stomach turn, and I had to talk to Sebastian about it. I had no intention of entering into a marriage with him if he was capable of behaving like that again. God knows what he would do if I left the cap off the toothpaste. Fuck the housekeeper? It had to be addressed.

Leon and I noticed Bridgette was coming back from the restroom and stopped talking about the call. Bridgette had a knack for taking on the problems of people she cared about personally. I got it; she was loyal to her friends. But getting unsolicited advice from her was beyond annoying. I didn't need another nagging mother. Giving Bridgette limited information about my problems with Sebastian was the best way to be friends with her.

After we finished our drinks, Bridgette suggested taking a ferry over to Mykonos to party for the evening. Hearing about the island and its all-night dance parties from her was enough to get us ready for an impromptu bachelorette party.

We left the bar and made our way up to our rooms to get ready. Leon decided that he would get me together again for the evening, like old times. He was still a bit hungover from earlier, but he was ready to party. After we got into our island attire, we met up with Bridgette in the lobby and headed to the dock in Athens, where we boarded a four-hour ferry ride to Mykonos.

We were overserved on the boat ride over, and after we disembarked, the three of us stumbled into to a rather strange bar that had people dancing in foam, which was spraying from the ceiling. There was crazy Greek dance music blasting, and foam was oozing onto the patrons on the dance floor. It was fun to dance in, but it was a mess. I had foam in places that were unmentionable. A few hours and several cocktails later, I realized it was starting to get late. I was sober enough to remember that Sebastian had told me he was going to call me later before he went to bed, and we still had four hours of travel time back to the hotel. I approached Leon, who had himself propped up against the bar.

"Don't you think we need to go?" I said, reminding him what Sebastian had told me earlier about calling me.

"Don't trip, girl. He knows who you're with. Besides, it's good for him if he calls you and you don't answer the phone," Leon said with a laugh.

"He might think something's happened to us, Leon," I said, concerned.

"Gina, it took four damn hours to get here. See that guy standing over there? I'm going to get with him, and you're going to call your nasty man and tell him where you're at," Leon said, laughing as he looked over at his prey for the night.

"I don't know where he's staying, Leon," I replied, frustrated

"Well, girl, then that's a problem … Let's see if your man can keep his nasty dick in his pants for a few more hours and not get pissed-off at you later," Leon said before walking away from me toward the guy he had his eyes on.

I knew Leon had been overserved on the Sebastian drama, so I walked back over toward Bridgette, who was now talking to a guy. While we danced, foam was going up the inside of my dress. It was so gross. I leaned into her and started talking really loudly over the music, suggesting that we take the ferry back.

"Gina, we have to wait until 6:00 a.m. There are no more ferries tonight. We're here. Relax. You're fine," Bridgette yelled back, and we started dancing again.

I was worried that maybe Sebastian would come to my room looking for me when I didn't answer the phone. I started to wonder if Leon was moving over to team Bridgette now. I mean, he was kind of dismissive at the bar. I was in a foreign country, miles away from my hotel, dancing in foam, but it was fun, I have to admit.

At 6:00 a.m., the sun still had not yet come up, and we saw Leon doing the drunk shuffle under the still-flickering bar lights. Bridgette and I had passed out on chairs outside of the bar. We were sticky with stale foam, and our hair was a mess. The three of us were exhausted as we made the walk of shame back to the dock to board the ferry, hung over to high heaven. I passed out in my seat, actually.

When our ferry pulled into the dock in Athens, my head was thumping. We got back to our hotel around 11:00 a.m. Bridgette headed to her room with her head hung to the floor, and Leon and I got to our room. The only thing either of us wanted to do was take a hot shower. I jumped in first, washing the stink and foam from my body. I wrapped my hair in a towel and put on my robe. Leon jumped up from the chair and entered the bathroom as I left.

I sat on my bed and stared at the flashing light on the phone. Then I checked the messages I knew were waiting for me. I had seven, and they were all from Sebastian.

11:01 p.m.—"Babe, I guess you're out on the town. I'll call back in an hour."

12:15 a.m.—"Hope you're having fun. I'll call you later."

3:30 a.m.—"Seriously, Gina?"

4:00 a.m.—"Where are you, Gina? Call me. I'm in room 444."

5:59 a.m.—"What the fuck, Gina?"

7:11 a.m.—"You didn't come home? That's fucking great." *Slam.*

8:00 a.m.—"Call me when you get this, babe. I'm worried about you."

I picked up the phone and made the call to Sebastian.

"Gina, this better be you," Sebastian said, aggravated

"Sebastian, I can—"

"Put Leon on the phone. I want to talk to him," Sebastian said in a cool tone.

I held the phone out to Leon, who had just come out of the bathroom after taking his one-minute de-funk shower.

"Girl, tell your king that this queen is tired, and she's going to bed to get her rest. I'll talk to his ass later. And put a sign on the door not to wake me up before five o'clock," Leon said to me as he got into bed, throwing the cover over his head.

I got back on the phone with Sebastian and told him Leon was out of it.

"I heard. Where have you been Gina?" Sebastian asked, concerned.

"We went to Mykonos to some foam bar," I replied casually,

"Mykonos! I wish you would have told me that yesterday, Gina," Sebastian said with a surprised inflection in his tone.

"Really, Sebastian? I didn't know the hotel you were staying in until just a few minutes ago. Not my problem I couldn't call you," I replied, aggravated.

"Okay, babe, I guess you need to go to bed," Sebastian replied, giving up.

"Sebastian, I need to ask you a question … The video girl, when did you break it off with her?" I asked inquisitively.

"Two months ago. Why, Gina?" he replied, disinterested in furthering the conversation.

"You used her to get back at me for some reason," I said passively.

"She was never my girlfriend, Gina," he replied, dismissively.

"But you used both of us," I said, upset.

"It's never going to happen again, Gina," he said somberly.

"I need you to break it off forever," I demanded.

"Will that make you feel better? Is that what you want? I'll do it. Come to my room. I'm in 444," he said, giving in to my request.

I got ready and took the elevator down to Sebastian's room. I was laser-focused on getting this video girl thing sorted with him. I felt anxious when I got to his room. I made a fist and knocked slowly three times. I was surprised, when the door opened, to see Rick greet me, putting his arms around me.

"G, it's great to see you. Marrying my ignorant brother, huh?"

I entered the room. Sebastian was sitting in a chair near the phone.

"Make the call, Bas," Rick said pointedly to Sebastian.

Sebastian picked up the phone and started placing a call to Los Angeles. I was nervous, as he was dialing the number from a cocktail napkin, but happy that I would be talking to the girl who flipped her hair in my face at that infamous video shoot.

"Laura, hey, it's Sebastian … Yeah, hey listen, I wanted to tell you that it's over between us for good. I'm getting married, and—"

I walked over and took the phone from his hand. "Laura? Funny, I never knew your name. I only knew you as the video girl. That day you flipped your hair in my face in DC, I forgive you for doing it only because you seem to lack manners. You'll never see my guy again, you can be assured of it," I said in a flat tone. Then I handed the phone back to Sebastian with a look of disgust.

"She's the love of my life, Laura. I wish you well. Take care," Sebastian said, and then he hung up the phone. I don't think he let

Laura get a word in edgewise, and I didn't give her a chance to say anything to me.

Sebastian was subdued as I asked him to give me the napkin and his little black book. He looked at me oddly when I asked for his address book, but I didn't back down. I said, "Give it to me."

I was guessing that he had one just like Chip had on tour. I recalled Chip adding a girl's name to his little black book the night before we got high on opium, making some crude comment about "revisiting that later," and it stuck with me. I remember thinking, *What a jerk.* In Europe, I saw that Rick had one like Chip's. I didn't think much of it until I reflected later on the odd similarities between those three during the tour.

Not to my surprise, Sebastian went to his suitcase and pulled out a book that was labeled *R. F. A.* Rick, looking worried, said, "Bas, don't give her the book, man."

Sebastian handed it to me, and I flipped through it, noticing that he had girls cataloged by city and not by their names. Each girl had a star rating next to her phone number. I looked under the *L*'s.

"Wow, Las Vegas Nicky has a five star rating with *B.J.* next to it. I guess she's really good at blackjack, huh, Bas?" I said, tossing the book sideways at him really hard with very little emotion. I held on to the cocktail napkin from the Rainbow Bar and Grill in Los Angeles that had Laura's name scribbled on it in eyeliner.

Rick's wife Alana had been right when we'd spoken in London on Sebastian's birthday. She'd told me that Sebastian and Rick were party boys. I hadn't believed it until I saw this "ready for action" book. He had so many girls to choose from.

"It's your choice what you do with your book of girls. I'm not going to deal with it," I told him with bit of an attitude. I was pissed that he had it with him in Greece after having just asked me to marry him.

Sebastian, with a dejected look, jumped up from his chair, grabbed the metal trash can next to the desk in one hand, and, holding his girly book in the other, flung open the balcony door. He threw the trash can outside in a huff and then held up the book and started to tear it apart. He took some matches that were sitting on a table and lit what remained of the book on fire, looking at me with cold eyes while he did this. He threw the burning notebook hard into the trash can. Rick was standing there with his mouth agape watching him do this. I went over and tossed the wrinkled napkin with Laura's number on it into the fire. That was the only number I really cared about anyway.

"I want you, no one else, Gina," he said with major attitude. I assumed that they were both embarrassed that I had figured out their little game of bullshit.

Standing on the balcony, looking at Rick and Sebastian in disgust, I added seven declarations to my wedding contract rider. Number one, if he cheated on me again, I was finished; that included getting blow jobs from their party girls on tour. Number two, he and Rick could no longer speak Greek around me unless their mother was in the room. Number three, I needed him to stay off the road while he was going through rehab; Rick was actually in agreement on this one. Number four, no more ex-girlfriends at video shoots. Number five, no more pills or coke. Number six, Lacey would always have gainful employment on their tours. Number seven, if he hurt me physically, I was gone, and if we had a child, I would take the kid with me. These were my seven deadly sins, and they were all nonnegotiable.

Sebastian had a few things to add to my rider. "Okay, Gina, one, your tour days are over. I'm shutting that down, showgirl. You're at home raising my kid. Two, if I need you in a city that I'm in when we're on tour, you bring my child with you. Three, don't ever throw Tiger's name in my face again like you did yesterday." He spoke sternly and seemed a bit pissed off, actually.

"Gina, how did you come to figure out about the girls? Nobody knew about that," Rick asked, turning with a confused look on his face toward Sebastian.

"Girls with laminated passes? Four in every city? You should have known better, Rick," I replied matter-of-factly.

I'd finally figured out why they spoke Greek in front of me. It was code; they were arranging girls to come to the shows so they could get sucked-off in their dressing rooms while Leon was busy doing Lacey's and my makeup for the shows. I figured out at that moment that this was why he'd hired Leon in the first place, to keep me occupied and away from his deviant behavior. When Alana told me about the boys' pile of party girls in London, it started making sense. I quickly reflected back on the girls I recalled seeing backstage with laminated passes—fan club managers, I was told. These girls didn't have the cloth passes usually given out to groupies by the road crew. The "lam girls" always came in fours. There was one for Chip, one for Rick, and one for Sebastian. Their drummer, Marcus, never partied on tour, but they always had a "spare" in the wings, and one of them would get a second helping. Rick, Chip, and Sebastian were thick as thieves on that tour, and their party girls had been prearranged in front of my face in Greek. I thought it was clever, but I was pissed the fuck off at him for doing it.

"You won't mention this to Alana, will you, Gina?" Rick asked, worried.

I assured Rick that I had no desire to relive his road stories with anyone, and that included his wife. Besides, Alana was already dialed in on Rick's infidelities; there was no need to mention it to her. She was able to turn a blind eye to this nonsense. I wasn't.

Since the three of us were being so open and honest with each other, I wanted to ask one final question of Sebastian. "How many blow jobs did you get on the 'Wait Tour,' Sebastian?" I asked calmly, awaiting the magic number that would follow. He looked at Rick for help, knowing they'd both gotten busted and that he may as well confess.

"About ten, but I never saw it as cheating on you, Gina," he replied, attempting to justify his actions.

"It is cheating, Sebastian, and now you both know," I replied sternly.

With truth serum spilling out all over the room, the boys and I were having our post-"Wait Tour" come-to-Jesus meeting. Sebastian paused and asked how far I'd made it with Tiger.

"As far as dinner the night I met him with you, Sebastian," I replied firmly. Looking over at Rick, I wanted to confront him about the video shoot, because he had known they were using Sebastian's ex-girlfriend Laura for it. "And by the way, it was really messed up that you allowed that video thing to happen in DC, Rick. You knew your brother and I were having issues." I was aggravated.

Rick insisted that he'd had no idea they were using Laura, but that he would have put a stop to it if he had. Knowing that Sebastian couldn't fart on that tour without him knowing about it, there was no way I believed him. I knew he was lying.

The three of us were getting our post-tour issues out in the open, that included them lecturing me about leaving the tour in DC the way I did. Neither one of them was happy about that, because it had left them an embarrassing mess to clean up. I really didn't care what they deemed embarrassing. I'd been humiliated by what Sebastian did to me at that video shoot.

"Sebastian, you really hurt me. Are we straight on this issue?" I said, really upset.

"Yeah, Gina, we're straight. I never intended to hurt you like that," Sebastian said as he walked over and took my hand and put his arms around my waist. "Rick, I need some time."

Rick put his hand on Sebastian's back and quietly left the balcony, apologizing to me on the way out.

"I can't function without you. I was messed up, G," Sebastian said with his head buried in my shoulder.

I pulled back from him and brought my hands to his face. "I know you're working hard to stay off the pills," I said as he put his arms around me and sighed.

Sebastian had told me after we reconnected that he had checked into a drug treatment facility the day after Leon called him. He wasn't done with his treatment—he'd paused it to meet me in Athens—but he was going back in after we got married. Our honeymoon would be one night spent in Greece, and then I would return to London with him so he could check back in to his drug treatment facility after Christmas. There would be no visitations for about a month. This is what I agreed to when I said yes to marrying him. His sobriety was the most important thing in our relationship. If I had a sober Sebastian, I had everything. He was thoughtful and affectionate, with his soul wide open and expressing love, because now he was sober. We had a connection like no two other people in the world. We'd understood each other from the day we met, but we also fed off of each other. We each held the nuke codes when it came to pissing each other off. I, too, needed to do some work on myself not to push his buttons anymore.

"My mom is going to be happy when she finds out what's going on. She was really pissed off at me when we broke up," Sebastian said with a slight smirk.

He wanted to surprise his mom about us getting married. I didn't understand why he was keeping our wedding a secret from his parents, but this was who he was, my Mr. Mysterious. He was still the guy of limited information, but this is the Sebastian I fell in love with.

"We'll catch up later when my parents get here. We're going to dinner to surprise them," Sebastian said with a small laugh and a devilish smile plastered on his face.

I was ready to leave Sebastian's room and head over to Bridgette's room so we could do some dress shopping when he said, "Babe, I'm having someone come to your room soon with some clothes. You and Bridgette get what you need for tomorrow."

Bridgette and I had made plans the night before to go shop for a wedding dress, but this was way better than trying to find something last minute. I asked him if he would send them to Bridgette's room, thanking him before I left.

"Let's meet back here at seven o'clock. Invite Leon and Bridgette to dinner with my parents." Just as I got to the door, he said with a smile, "See if you can stay in Athens today."

I walked to Bridgette's room down the hall and knocked. She answered the door barley awake and a complete mess. Bridgette was still hung over to high heaven from last night's festivities. She let me in, and I walked over to her bed and lay down, looking at her with my head on the other pillow.

"We're in luck. Sebastian is sending someone here with clothes for us to pick out," I said, as she got back into bed.

"I love him, Gina. I actually love him right now," Bridgette said as she put her pillow over her head and went back to sleep. I lay next to her thinking about our fun times in New York, our slumber parties spent talking about guys and dating. I really saw Bridgette as my sister more than a friend. She always had my back, no matter what. I wondered if, after I married Sebastian, I would ever see her again. New York was starting to seem like a distant memory to me.

Thirty minutes passed by, and then there was a knock on the door. When I opened it, I was greeted by a very impatient man with a rolling rack of dresses. He started speaking Greek to me.

"Bridgette, do you speak Greek?" I asked, looking over at her with the pillow over her head as the man rolled the rack into the room.

Bridgette took the pillow that was over her head and put it on the floor. *"Hai portato i vestiti?"*

The man looked over at Bridgette and replied, frustrated, *"miloún italiká"*

"Fanculo! Gina, I don't speak *Greco,"* Bridgette said, aggravated.

"Greco! Greco! Italiká … gamó," the man said, frustrated.

There was an international thing going on between them, and I wasn't going to get mixed up in it. Bridgette, annoyed with the man, tore out of bed and suggested I call Sebastian. I had a better idea. Placing a call to the front desk, I asked to be connected to Rick's room. Luckily, Alana answered the phone, and I asked her to come to room 433 to help us pick out dresses and told her that we were dealing with a language-barrier thing.

"I'll be there in five minutes," Alana said, and she hung up the phone.

Alana came right over, leaving her son, David, with Rick. I hadn't seen her since Sebastian's birthday, and that was nine months ago. We hugged and started to catch up, but the man with the dresses was getting more impatient. Alana stepped in and took over the conversation with him. I turned to Bridgette and told her that Alana was my Greek secret weapon.

Bridgette caught on right away and replied, "Maybe you better learn Greek too, Gina. You'll know what's going on with him." She had been dialed in on Sebastian's behavior way before I was, but being loyal to her friends was her strong suit. Bridgette had always set me straight on Sebastian's behavior, giving me unsolicited advice about him when we were dating, but she was also very loyal to Sebastian in her own way. She would never allow someone to speak bad of him in her presence. She could herself, but if you didn't know him and talked smack, you would suffer the consequences.

The three of us tried on dresses, and I had selected the one I wanted. I told Bridgette that maybe we better include Leon. I called up to my room, and Leon answered.

"Your ass better not be in jail," he said when he picked up the phone. I laughed and told him that we were trying on dresses for the wedding in Bridgette's room and asked if he would like to come and approve my selection. He stated that he would need to approve whatever it was that I selected but that I had to come to him, because he was incapable of leaving his bed. Mykonos had gotten the better of him.

I put on the dress, and the four of us took the elevator to my room. I opened the door, and Leon was just getting up. "Girl, turn. Oh, I like it on you, but don't you think you might want to look a little more, um … virginish? That dress screams, 'I've been around the block a few times, and I know what a dick looks like; don't let the color of this dress fool you.' But I do like it, girl," Leon stated very matter-of-factly.

We were all in stitches at Leon's comment. Alana explained what Leon had said in Greek to the dress man, who blushed. Bridgette thought the short minidress was appropriate for marrying a rock star. Leon suggested that I get two dresses, one for the more formal vows in front of his parents and the "dick dress" for after the wedding.

The five of us headed back to Bridgette's room, where we'd left the other dress selections. Leon walked over to the rack with fierce determination and began tearing through them.

"It's a good thing you got my ass out of bed. You pick that short-ass thing to say I do in, and his mom be sitin' there thinkin' you're a hussy. Here … go, girl. Put this on," Leon said, handing me a floor-length, fitted dress that was more appropriate.

I made the final selection of my two dresses, and Bridgette made hers. I then announced that Sebastian had invited us all to dinner. Leon looked at the dress man and said with a sigh, "You need to bring us more dresses and shoes."

Alana told the man what Leon had said, and the dress man smiled and made an urgent call back to his store. Alana told us that more dresses would be arriving in thirty minutes. Leon went upstairs to lay back down and said to call him when the second delivery arrived.

When the new dresses arrived, I called Leon, and he came back to Bridgette's room in a more chipper mood. He went directly to the new rack of clothes, picking one for each of us to wear that the evening, critiquing each of us as we walked out of the bathroom after trying them on. I don't think the dress man had figured we would be buying this many outfits and shoes, but he seemed very pleased. We made our selections. The dress man tallied up the bill and left a credit card receipt for Sebastian.

After the dress man left, we went back to our respective rooms to take naps and then get ready for dinner with Sebastian's parents. Leon and I were carrying my dress selections back to the room when I asked if he needed to buy some clothes. Leon told me Sebastian had left him a message saying that he had already taken care of his wedding attire. Leon told me in a serious tone that he would be wearing an electric-blue speedo on my wedding day.

I had gotten back into bed when there was a knock on the door. A bellman had delivered a garment bag for Leon. "Your speedo just got delivered," I said, hanging it on the back of the door.

"Who made it?" Leon asked seriously.

"Armani," I replied, knowing it wasn't a speedo.

"There better be some damn shoes in that bag," Leon said as he pulled the cover over his head.

"There are—two pairs to go with two suits," I replied as I unzipped the bag to check.

"Girl, that man is on point," Leon said, and he went back to sleep.

At five thirty, Leon and I woke up. He got into the shower, and I called Bridgette, who was getting up from her nap as well. She asked if I wanted to get ready in her room, which I said I did. I made a call to Alana's room to see if the boys' parents had made it to town yet. She said Sebastian and Rick were downstairs having a drink with them, but she was waiting for David to wake up from his nap before going down to join them. Rick had told her about Sebastian wanting to surprise his parents, and she thought it was a crazy idea. But she was excited about the wedding and having me as her sister-in-law.

"It's really lonely for me without Rick when he tours, Gina. I'm so happy you're coming to England. We live so close to Sebastian. I can't wait till you have your own kids; it really makes dealing with the touring more tolerable when you have a little one who needs looking after." Alana said. She was happy that Sebastian and I were getting married. If I could get Bridgette on the same page, it would be a perfect day.

I had my new prewedding outfit in hand and went off to Bridgette's room. Leon came down about an hour later. He finished our makeup, and at 6:55 p.m. I called Sebastian to tell him we were ready. He told me that his parents and Rick's family had already left the hotel and said to meet him in the lobby. He had a car waiting for us. Leon, Bridgette, and I went down to the lobby, and we were greeted by my guy, who I had not seen dressed up in several months. His long hair accented his nice black shirt, his tight-fitting jeans that showcased his hatred for wearing underwear, and his boots, which added extra height to his already six-foot-three stature. He looked at me with fire in his eyes, the same fire I remember seeing the first day I met him. We stared at each other, and Sebastian took my hands and gave me a kiss on the cheek, saying, "I know this sounds crazy, but will you marry me?"

I melted right there on the spot. I smiled at him and said, "I know this sounds crazier, but yes, I'll marry you." He grabbed my face, and we made out in the lobby with people staring at us.

Bridgette walked to the car when she couldn't get our attention. Leon snickered as he walked by us and said, "I didn't bring the makeup bag, Sebastian."

Sebastian pulled back, and we walked to the car, where Bridgette and Leon were waiting for us. Leon suggested again that Sebastian keep his hands off of me because he didn't have his makeup case. Sebastian replied, "I heard you. I'll do my best."

In the car on our way to the restaurant, Sebastian gave us a run-down of Operation "Shock the Hell out of My Parents," saying he was going to have me wait and hide in the restaurant. On cue, I would surprise his mom.

We arrived at the restaurant, and I was nervous. I could tell Sebastian was too, but he, Bridgette, and Leon got out of the car and walked into the restaurant. I waited a few minutes before I went inside. When I saw that the coast was clear, I stood behind a large plant toward the back of the restaurant, close enough to the table they were sitting at that I could hear what was going on but still well hidden from the table so they couldn't see me. Sebastian walked over to his mom and gave her a hug. He introduced his parents to Bridgette and asked them if they remembered Leon. They all said their hellos, and I could hear them speaking. Sebastian took his seat and acted like nothing was going on. His mom started speaking in Greek, but Sebastian politely asked her not to do that with guests at the table.

Sebastian turned to his mother, paused, and said, "*Mitera*, Dad, I asked you to come here because I have something I need to tell you." He turned to Leon and took his hand. "*Mitera*, Dad ... Leon and I are in love ... and I'm gay." Rick and Bridgette started busting up laughing. The boy's parents didn't, and Athene started yelling at Sebastian in Greek.

"Sebastian Adonis Rolland, *sas boke mitéres kardiá sas*." (You broke your mother's heart.)

Sebastian's dad, Richard, who was shaking his head, yelled at him, "This was the family emergency you called me to Greece for? You're gay? I don't believe it, Sebastian." Richard looked at him in disbelief; he was not buying into any of his son's nonsense.

Leon pulled his hand back from Sebastian rolled it over his head, turning away from him. "Sebastian, you know you ain't right."

Rick, Bridgette, and Alana were all laughing hysterically, and his parents were getting more aggravated by the minute. Sebastian turned to his mother, put his arm around her chair, and said seriously, "*Mitera*, I'm getting married."

I had been standing off to the side, hearing most of the conversation going on, when I saw Sebastian lean into his mother. I took that as my cue and walked up to the table behind her. Richard heaved a sigh of relief when I came into view and smiled, putting my hands on Athene's shoulders. She was startled and turned around. When Athene saw me, she jumped out of her chair and started crying.

"Gina! Sebastian *egó tha sas timorísei argótera*." (Sebastian, I will punish you later.) She put her arms around me, smiling, as Richard called the waiter over and ordered a bottle of Ouzo for the table.

Leon was happy to get up and move down a chair away from Sebastian. I took the open chair, leaned over to Sebastian, and asked how it had gone over. "Perfect," he said.

Athene wanted to order food for the table. By now the bottle of Ouzo had arrived and was flowing mostly in the direction of Rick and his father. Sebastian did one shot for the celebration but then went back to drinking water. Bridgette and Leon were having a great time, and it made me very happy that my best friends were blending into Sebastian's family as if to be a part of it. We all had a great time laughing while we waited for the food to arrive.

Rick and Leon were getting caught up from the tour and telling Bridgette about the crazy escapades that took place on the bus, with Alana rolling her eyes in my direction. Rick, who was seated next to Bridgette and seemed like he was flirting with her, said, "We're leasing a jet for the next tour. Want to work for us?"

Bridgette, unimpressed, told him that she loved her job but that she would think about it. Bridgette wasn't easily impressed by rock stars. She worked in first class and interacted with them on a daily basis. They were her least favorite people to deal with. Leon and I looked at each other and had the same thought: *that would be a fun tour.*

But Sebastian caught wind of Rick's comment and my reaction to it, and he turned away from his mother in midconversation and said, "Your touring days are over, babe." He put his arm around my neck and, holding on to my shoulder, pulled me into him for a kiss on my head, leaving me disappointed.

After dinner, we took two cars back to the hotel. Everyone wanted to celebrate in the bar, but Sebastian wanted a few minutes alone. We walked outside and sat on a bench. He seemed melancholy.

"Gina, I want tomorrow to be special for us. You've never had me sober. I'm going to give you every part of me that you've never had before. I want you to think about that all night while I'm thinking about you." He sat there looking at the expression on my face after that comment, which was one of shock. We got up from the bench, and he brought his hands to my face and gave me the most lustful kiss I'd ever gotten from him. He pulled back. "I love you more than anything in this world, Gina, and so does my family. If I do something that you don't like, tell me. Don't leave me like you did in DC. That was pretty fucking hurtful."

And what he did to me in DC wasn't? I looked at him, shocked by his comment. His behavior was emotional, bordering on the dramatic. I hadn't seen this side of him before.

We walked back into the bar area, where he adopted a more up-beat and masculine demeanor. Our group was in full cocktail swing. A few hours later, I was talking with the boy's parents when I saw Bridgette walk by. I grabbed her. It was getting late, and I decided I wanted to hang with her and Leon alone. The three of us had the same idea. We decided to stay in the same room together for one last slumber party.

I walked over to Sebastian, who was speaking to Rick and Alana, and told him I was going back to my room. He took my hands and said, "May the gods let me live through the night just to see you to-morrow." It gave me butterflies. I kissed him goodnight and walked back to my room with Bridgette and Leon.

I stared back at my guy, just like I had done the day I'd met him, and we didn't take our eyes off of each other. I took my hand and blew him a kiss when I got to the elevator. He reached up to catch it, putting it to his heart and smiling. Bridgette started crying when we got on the elevator.

"B, why are you crying?" Leon asked, shaking his head,

"I really like him now, Gina," Bridgette said as Leon rolled his eyes.

We got to our room and started changing into pajamas. Bridgette borrowed some of mine. We realized we all had pajamas with *NYC* printed on the pants and laughed at ourselves. We took pictures in our New York pj's, hit the mini bar for snacks, and jumped into bed. Leon suggested we play some truth or dare before going to sleep.

"Bridgette, truth or dare?"

"Truth," Bridgette replied, tearing open a chip bag.

"What happened to Lou from the bar?" Leon asked.

"We broke up," Bridgette responded. "Gina, truth or dare?"

"Wait, hold up. You can't do that … what happened?" Leon said.

"He was boring. We broke up about a month ago. I thought you knew," Bridgette replied, crunching chips.

"No, I didn't. Been kind of busy moving and dealing with Sebastian. Now I got to find a new roommate," Leon said, disappointed.

"Leon, come to London. Sebastian is going back into rehab after our wedding," I said with enthusiasm, grabbing one of Bridgette's chips.

"Don't you need to check with your man first?" Leon replied inquisitively.

"Leon, you and Bridgette are my best friends in the entire world. Sebastian loves you both," I said. I told them about Sebastian's sobriety and what was going to happen with him over the course of the next month. I told them that I had no intention of giving up my apartment in New York. I was going to keep it for a while and still pay my rent just in case things got crazy with his pill addiction. Leon was delighted to hear that news, and the pressure was off to find another roommate.

I wanted Leon to come to my new home after his Christmas trip to Italy. I wanted him to have an easier transition to me not being in New York 24-7. Leon was the one who had really picked up my pieces after I left the tour, and he'd ended up being the one responsible for Sebastian and I getting back together. Leon and I had both managed to save our money from the tour to live in New York, so rent wasn't the issue. It was the companionship that forged our relationship. We both needed each other. I was his art project, and he was my big brother.

Leon said he would stay on with me for a few weeks while Sebastian was in rehab. He wanted to inquire about getting some fashion gigs with Emily (the Stitch Bitch) in London while he was there also. Leon was transitioning into the world of fashion; that was where his true talent lay. He was able to take pieces, put them together, and make them work. Leon had an eye for fashion. Bridgette chimed in and said that she could work the London route and would have to leave New York if we were both living in England.

As we lay there talking, Bridgette asked Leon if he'd spoken to Walter lately, and that opened a conversation about Walter and Jewels, who were now expecting a baby. That made Walter's father delighted. Leon said he didn't see much of Walter these days but spoke to him a few times a week. Bridgette told us that Jewels was really wrapped up in the socialite life now, using her given name, Julia, and hyphenating her last name like the rest of the upper-west-side, wannabe-Kennedy crowd. She was Julia Renee Jourdan-Woodrow, made official by fine, linen stationery purchased at Crane letter shop on Fifth Avenue.

Jewels really had changed her persona after she married Walter. Ms. Julia had distanced herself from her old friends soon after they got married and was running in more "suitable" social circles now, even leaving her job at the airlines.

"She's French," Bridgette said. "What did you expect?" I knew Bridgette said that out of hurt; they were best friends.

A few weeks before Leon and I had taken off for Greece, we'd tried giving Jewels a baby shower at the Christopher Street apartment, but Jewels had the nerve to tell Bridgette, her best friend of several years, that her socialite friend Katherine Kendal Bride-McDavis had offered to host a couple's shower in her "more suitable, perfectly appointed, upper-west-side home." That pissed Bridgette off. You don't say stuff like that to your best friend, who is like a sister to you. Putting social status over friendship always equals bullshit.

Leon, Bridgette, and I declined the invite to the baby shower but did manage to send over a proper, not to mention very expensive, gift to the upper-snotty-side Bride-McDavis apartment: a sexy, leather-clad male stripper holding a leather whip in one hand and a designer leather onesie just like his in the other for the respectable parents' soon-to-be-born new baby. Jewels took a Frenchie attitude toward our thoughtful gift and decided that she would never be able to speak to us again from the sheer embarrassment. "Whatever, Jewels McCunty-Woodrow," summed up our attitude about the whole thing. She should just get over it. Walter had; he thought that shit was funny.

Reliving this story with Leon and Bridgette was painfully exhausting, and all I could think about was what Sebastian had said to me earlier in the evening about getting it from him really good on my wedding night. I told Bridgette how happy I was, and she started getting teary eyed.

Leon said, "If you two bitches don't stop crying, I'm never going to get my beauty rest. I'm happy for you, Gina, but if you knew the shit I went through to get you here ... Goodnight bitch." Then he turned out the light on the nightstand.

"We love you Leon," Bridgette and I said at the same time.

"I love you too ... Bitches have my heart. I'll be real with you on that." He said the latter part to himself, but he wanted us to hear him say it.

In Your Eyes

Waking up to a bright and sunny morning, I quietly took the phone and went out on the balcony to order room service. Bridgette and Leon were still sleeping. I was still processing that I was actually getting married and made a call to Sebastian's room, nervous to hear his voice before he answered the phone.

"You know, when I woke up this morning, I had the most incredible feeling about you," I said as I sat back in the balcony chair, twisting the phone cord with my hand.

"Yeah? And what was that?" he replied, interested.

"I'm getting married today. What do you think about that?" I said, playfully.

"I think he's the luckiest man in the world," Sebastian replied in a serious tone.

"Is it real?" I asked. The reality was setting in that I was getting married.

"It was a long road, Gina. I'll look into your eyes in a few hours and tell you how much I love you, baby," Sebastian replied like a man in love with his dream girl.

After hanging up with my soon-to-be rock-star husband, I was smitten like a little kitten, sitting on the balcony and taking in the warm sun. Room service arrived with breakfast, and the attendant set up the table outside. It was a beautiful day. It was a warm seventy degrees, and there was a light breeze blowing. Leon, awoken by the smell of fresh bacon that had drifted into the bedroom, walked out to the balcony with a notepad. He started pouring coffee into one of the empty cups sitting on the table.

"Good morning, sunshine," I said to Leon, who had just put on his sunglasses.

"Good morning, Mrs. Roland. Lord, that reminds me, I need to have the talk with your nasty man today before I set you free," Leon replied with a snicker as he sat down. He took a plate and put bacon on it. He was making notes on a schedule he had written out on a hotel notepad and started going over the day's activities. "At one o'clock, we have hair and makeup,"

Bridgette walked out onto the balcony in a bouncy and jubilant mood wearing sunglasses. She poured herself a cup of coffee and sat down with her feet propped up on an empty chair next to Leon.

Leon continued with the wedding schedule. "At two o'clock, you and B will be getting dressed." Leon looked at Bridgette's feet. "You need a pedicure, Miss Thing. We have the photographer at four, at four thirty I need to put my foot in Sebastian's ass, and then at five I'll be walking you to your nasty man." Leon again looked over at Bridgette. "And at 5:01 p.m., Bridgette will be crying on cue, girl." Leon laughed as Bridgette hit him on the arm playfully. "I need to figure out dress two for later. What do you think, B, right after dinner?" Leon asked as they started putting food on their plates from the communal breakfast foods in the center of the table.

"I say right before. We won't see Gina after dinner; she hasn't been with him yet," Bridgette said, taking a bite of bacon.

Leon was taking a sip of coffee and choked. "You mean to tell me you he hasn't slipped you any since we been here?" Leon asked, looking at me in shock. I explained that Sebastian wanted to wait on that until after we got married. Leon raised an eyebrow at Bridgette and put down his fork. "B, these two used to go at it five or six times a day." He looked at me in disbelief. "Damn, Gina, you're serious?" I shook my head yes. "Girl, this man has changed. I hope he can still get it up after all the pills and blow that man has done." He laughed as he picked up his fork and continued eating his breakfast.

The wedding day for me was not stressful. I took a shower, and at noon, Bridgette and I started getting ready. By the time four thirty rolled around, I was staring at the clock. Leon had left the room to check on Sebastian, to make sure we wouldn't cross paths in the hall, and to have the "Leon's expectations" talk with him, which probably consisted of Louis bags and other designer nonsense.

After about twenty minutes, Leon called back to the room, letting Bridgette know the coast was clear and that the photographer had just finished photos with Sebastian's family. Bridgette looked at me and asked if I was ready. She told me with tears in her eyes how happy she was for me and said that even though Sebastian put me through a major ordeal, she had seen a side of him with his parents that had let her know he was a great guy. I was surprised by her change in attitude toward him, and it made me very happy.

We headed down to the hotel's wedding area and then to a tiny holding space outside facing the makeshift altar on the hotel's restaurant balcony, which Sebastian had privately reserved for the day. Traditional Greek music had started, performed by a local Greek ensemble. I saw that Sebastian and Rick had just come to the altar waiting for the ceremony to start and seemed highly annoyed with the selection of the music of their motherland. I caught them rolling their eyes at each other after glancing at the musicians.

Leon came into the tiny room Bridgette and I were waiting in and asked me if I was ready to go. Bridgette took a breath, looked at me, and said, "This is it, your last train stop." She gave me a hug and left the holding area to join Sebastian and Rick. Leon and I were looking at each other when she left.

"Are you ready?" Leon asked, and I nodded my head yes. Leon took my arm and interlocked it with his. "I had the talk with him and put my foot in his ass a few minutes ago." We both snickered. Then he began leading me to the altar.

Being a punk rock girl at heart, I had no intention of walking to "Here Comes the Bride." I wanted to walk to the song that Sebastian had written for me, though I hadn't told Sebastian of my plan to do that. I had had some mixed feelings about the song at first, since Laura, the girl he cheated on me with, was used in the video, but I talked it over with Bridgette, and she said, "Don't give her the power to take that away from you, Gina." I agreed. Bridgette was right.

When Sebastian saw me walking with Leon, he smiled, tilted his head, and started tearing up. I smiled at him. Leon took my hand and placed it into Sebastian's, giving him a pat on the back and saying, "She's my girl, and you better take care of her, Sebastian,"

"I will, Leon. I promise," Sebastian said as he hugged Leon for an extended period of time, causing Sebastian to get very emotional.

Everyone was taken aback by their exchange, and Bridgette started crying. She was a bucket of tears. Leon took his seat next to Sebastian's mother and was bawling his eyes out. It was stress tears from the weeks of keeping secrets to get us to this point. Athene took Leon's head to her shoulder and let him cry. The wedding coordinator had to pause the ceremony for a minute until everyone collected themselves, including Sebastian, who turned his back to everyone to compose himself. Rick put a hand on his shoulder. Leon and Sebastian's exchange had had a chain effect on everyone else. Sebastian turned back around and glanced over at Rick, who asked if he was okay.

The officiate preforming our vow exchange asked in Greek if he should proceed. Sebastian's mother stood up and said, "*Na synechisei.*" (Continue.) Since vows were not exchanged in Greek marriages, we simply put rings on each other's fingers and said a few words to each other.

"I'll love you till the other side of time, Gina," Sebastian said, putting the ring on my finger with tears filling his eyes again.

"I love you, my Greek god," I replied, placing his ring on his finger with a smile and then wiping away my tears with a small laugh.

Sebastian leaned in close to my ear so nobody could hear him. "That makes me hard when you call me that. Look."

I looked down at his member, letting out a laugh, and everyone wondered what he'd said. We knew it could never be repeated. And with his comment about being hard, we were married. It took two minutes.

Before we left the makeshift altar, Sebastian made an announcement. "I'm going to kiss my new bride. *Mitera*, close your eyes." Sebastian leaned me back and passionately kissed me, putting his head into my chest before he pulled me back up to my feet. If this was any indication of what was coming later, I would be in for one hell of a night. We walked down the aisle smiling and holding hands. As we walked over to a ledge draped in flowers to take wedding photos, Leon whispered into my ear that he needed to touch up my makeup and that he thought it was better to wait until cocktail hour to change into the "dick dress." It wasn't the appropriate time, especially since Sebastian's mother was in shock after witnessing her son's lip-lock with me in front of "the gods."

Sebastian and I took photos with the sun setting in the background. A nice, warm Athens breeze had set in for the evening by the time we rejoined the wedding party. They were already seated for dinner on the outside balcony dining area. The table was dressed in white linen and beautifully lit with candelabras draped in flowers and Irish greenery, chosen by Sebastian on behalf of my heritage since I'd opted not to hold a wedding bouquet.

Sebastian and I took our seats, and Rick took the knife to his water glass, taping it three times. He stood up with his son David in his arms.

"Well, let me get this started. Bas, I was there the day you met Gina. I knew the minute you saw her that you'd gotten hit with the stick. Thank you, Leon, for bringing these two back together. What you did was a beautiful thing. Gina, he's still my ignorant brother, but I love him. I've been waiting to say this for a while: Welcome to the family, Gina." He then whispered into David's ear to say something.

"*Eviva!*" (Cheers!) David blurted out over the table, and everyone thought it was so cute to hear a four-year-old say cheers in Greek.

Leon, who was looking over at Bridgette, indicated to her that he wanted to be the next one to speak. As he stood up, everyone got silent. "Gina, Sebastian, where do I start?" He paused. "I could say that you both tested my patience with your love drama and theatrics, but I won't. What I will say to you, Gina, is this: you're my sister and my best friend." Leon started tearing up and put his hand on my back. "We've been through it. Sebastian and Gina have a special connection; I saw it more than anyone. Be in the same room with them for a few minutes and you can feel that love. It's real. And the love they have for one another will be around longer than any of us sitting at this table. You both are a mess, but I love you. Take care of her, Sebastian; you don't want Bridgette's mess to come and pay you any visits." He sat down, laughing, and then turned away from everyone, complaining the he had something in his eye. They were tears that he was trying to laugh away.

Sebastian got up from his chair, and I leaned over to Leon. We both hugged him, but he started fussing that we were making a scene. Bridgette and Alana started crying. Athene was wiping away her tears. She got up from her seat to get the waiter to bring over a tissue box for the table, and Leon grabbed the first one.

Bridgette stood up, and Sebastian, looking at her, slumped back in his chair. "*Rilassare* (relax), Sebastian. I'm not coming for you." Leon let out a loud laugh at her comment, covering his mouth with his tissue.

"Gina, the day you came to Christopher Street, I knew we would hit it off. I had to bust your balls a bit, but you took it. Gina and I are both smartasses that got each other right away. You're a beautiful person on the inside and out." She paused. "Gina and I were roommates when she met Sebastian. At first I had some reservations about her being with him, because she is my best friend, but I knew she was in love with him. Gina, I love you. I know your dad, and I know he would have loved to have been here today. My sister from another mister, I'm going to miss those slumber parties." She paused again to take a tissue from the box, dotting her eyes with it, and then turned to Sebastian with a *capo-di-tutti-capi* (boss-of-bosses) demeanor. "Gina will be forever loyal to you, Sebastian. Remember that," she said. Sebastian seemed visibly uncomfortable at the last part of her speech. Can't imagine why, really. Wink, wink.

I got up from my chair and hugged her. Bridgette was more than a friend. She'd been there for me, picking up my pieces when Sebastian shattered my heart just a few months earlier.

As I sat back down, I took Sebastian's hand and said, "Sebastian, my life was forever changed the day I met you in New York. Where we have been, what we've been through … I love you more than I am able to express in simple words. Sebastian Adonis Roland, my Greek god, I love you." I had just placed a kiss on his lips when a bolt of lightning streaked across the sky. It wasn't even raining. Athene proclaimed that it was a sign sent from Zeus blessing the marriage. She was happy the gods were showing their approval.

Leon jumped in his chair and turned to me with a stern look. "You need to leave that Greek god thing alone. I'm serious, Gina. You have the Lord chiming in on that one, and he don't play, girl."

I put my hand on Leon's back and said, "Okay."

Sebastian took my hand and pulled me into him, whispering into my ear, "Thank you, baby, for saying that to me in front of my family." He gave me a peck on the lips and then took command of the table. "Now I have something to say to my girl." He took my hand to his chest and looked me in the eyes. "Gina, you can be assured of one thing: you'll always have this." He placed my hand on his heart, saying, "I will love you till the other side of time, G." Then he sealed it with a kiss.

The waiter started to put premade plates in front of each guest, a meal consisting of traditional Greek foods. Ouzo flowed around the table for several hours, through the entire meal. After dinner, we didn't have a traditional wedding cake. Instead, hot tea and a plate of baklava and Greek cookies was served to each guest. When the others started to get up from the table and make their way over to the bar, Bridgette and I went upstairs, and I changed into the shorter dress. Then, after Bridgette stopped for a smoke, we headed back to our party. We joined Leon and Alana, who were talking outside. I noticed Sebastian was off in a corner outside speaking with Rick on a couch under a heat lamp. I walked toward them and snuck up behind Sebastian, putting my arms around his neck.

"Where did you go? … Oh! Damn, baby," Sebastian said, noticing I had changed out of my longer dress. He pulled me onto his lap and whispered into my ear, "I want to get out of here and inside of you." He had the look of the devil plastered on his face.

"I'll make sure I say goodbye to everyone before we go. Oh, by the way," I said, playing with his hair as I changed the subject, "I invited Leon to stay at your house after his trip to Milan. Is that okay?"

"It's not my house, Gina; it's our house. Absolutely he can stay on with you while I'm away. That would make me feel better about leaving, actually," Sebastian said, relieved.

"Aw, that is sweet. Sorry I didn't check with you first before I asked him," I said, putting my arms around his neck.

"Leon is family, G." Sebastian said. He looked over at Rick who got up to talk to his parents. I was sitting on his lap and felt him getting hard. He told me he wanted to go.

We got up and walked over to Leon, Alana, and Bridgette to say goodnight, telling them we were ready to hit the sheets. Leon laughed and teased me in my ear that he hoped his thing still worked. Sebastian and I walked over to bid pleasant dreams to his mom, who was holding David. Then he turned to his dad and Rick. We waived goodbye to everyone and headed to the elevator.

Sebastian leaned in close to my ear. "A night you will never forget. I hope you're ready for it."

As we got off the elevator and headed to Sebastian's room, he picked me up and carried me to the door, asking me to get the key out of his pants. I started laughing really hard, recalling the first night in New York when he'd had me fetch his key from his pants. Sebastian told me that he was serious. He said he wasn't going to put me down and I needed to get the key. I put my hand in his pants pocket, feeling his manhood extending as I got the key. I unlocked the door, and he kicked it open with his foot and took me over to the bed, where he laid me down. He went back to put the do-not-disturb tag on the door and then lay down next to me. He was observing me as if he were meeting me for the first time, taking his hand and moving it up the side of my face, drawing me in closer to him. We were interlocked and looking at each other.

"The air you exhale, I want to breath it in," he said in complete ecstasy, looking deep into my eyes.

"I love you so much, Sebastian. I always have," I replied.

"Baby, I just want to take time and look at you." His head moved slowly up to my neck. He began to breathe harder as he put his hand between my thighs, moving it up tenderly, stopping at my privates, and looking lustfully in my eyes. He unzipped the back of my dress.

His touch was soft and gentle, and his desire for me was different than I had remembered from the past. He started to take me out of the dress, and when I tried to assist, he said, "Let me do all of the work."

I started unbuttoning his shirt and started to go after the button of his pants. He turned over on his back and let me take them off. I was surprised to find he was wearing underwear. I assumed it was because he didn't want his *Mitera* to see his Greek assets bouncing around in his suit pants. He usually had a disdain for wearing them.

He had managed to wrangle me out of the skin-tight "dick dress" while I was on top of him, stating his preference for that one over the more formal dress I had worn for the vows. We were exploring each other when he said, "Relax and get comfortable." He put me on my back and never broke his gaze with me as he made his way downtown.

Placing a pillow under me when he got there, he took his hands and gently started spreading me open at the knees. Then he gently buried his face in my intimate business. He was taking his time teasing me, and that was working, because I started grabbing the sheets and making loud noises.

"I'm yours, baby, yours," I screamed out. I grabbed the sheets harder. "Baby, I'm coming." He went in faster with his tongue, making me moan louder until I climaxed. When I did, he took off his underwear. His eight-inch cock was fully hard when he entered me. He was kind enough not to give me time to catch my breath from my experience. I had the incredible feeling of having eight thick inches buried deep inside me after having the best orgasm of my life. He pulled the pillow out from under me and we went primal. The sounds coming from us ranged from "I missed you" to "fuck, oh fuck."

I was so wet from him; I could feel it on the sheets underneath me. And he was so hard that each time he pushed himself further into me, I screamed his name louder. He started passionately kissing me, shoving his snake further into my garden. Our hair was wet, our bodies dripping in perspiration, and the fire between us was intense.

Sebastian said, "Come with me, baby," and he positioned himself for a few good strokes, taking my left knee with him. On the final stroke, he said, "I love you so much," and we came together. He lay on top of my chest, putting his right arm around my back to bring us in tighter. We felt our bodies tingle as if they were one.

We stayed in that position for what seemed like forever. Finally, he said, "That's round one. We have a few more to go, and each round gets better. Let's take a shower." He extended his hand and led me to the bathroom.

Just as we got near the bathroom door, we heard laughing on the other side of it. Sebastian put his hand to my mouth, and walked near the door. "Leon, Bridgette! I'm giving you two seconds to leave." He opened the door, sticking his head out to see them both running down the hall laughing. "Seriously? It's our wedding night, assholes," he yelled, slamming the door and shaking his head. He put his arms around me. "What we have stays between us." I felt his manhood get bigger because it brushed between my thighs. "It's special, what we have, G. People want it, and I don't want to share it with anyone."

"Ok, my Greek god," I said lustfully, feeling his member getting harder near my passage.

"God, that makes me hard," he replied, ready for round two. He opened the shower door and turned on the water. We began making out as he led me into the shower, not checking the water temperature. He pulled me in as we our impatient hands roamed each other's bodies. He turned me to face the water with his arms snug around my waist, teasing me with his package on my backside. He inserted himself into me from behind, asking me to bend my legs a bit so he could get his number eight inside. Lukewarm water was hitting us, and Sebastian said he wanted to take a more romantic approach to the position, so he pulled out, and put me back to the wall and entered me again. I was feeling his thunder down under. He took his time, slowly and loving caressing my hair as he moved back and forth inside of me. He let out moans of pleasure—"Oh, G, you feel so good, baby"—as his hands moved all over my wet body.

Out of nowhere, he pulled me out of the shower and led back through the bedroom and onto the balcony, soaking wet. He took me out to a chaise lounge, where we proceeded to make love under the stars. It was raw and intense, in the manner typical of our old lovemaking days, which I happened to have enjoyed very much. When he said, "Let's sleep out here under the stars just like this," I was thinking, *No way, guy, everyone on the fifth floor will look down in the morning and see our business. I want to take a proper shower and go to bed, thank you very much.*

He did persuade me to stay out there for at least a few hours. We said things to each other that we had never said before, admitting that it had been love at first sight for us both. I lay curled up with my head on his chest. He told me that I was the only true love of his life, the only girl who really got him. I understood him completely but wondered if, had we not met through Lex, we would ever have met at all. I decided that we probably wouldn't have. I would never have attended a Tin Garden show, and he was not much into attending Broadway plays. Sebastian said that Lex and Stan were the ones who brought us together, but they also had a part in ripping us apart, unknowingly, of course.

We talked about all the crazy stuff we did on tour, until I fell asleep. At about 3:00 a.m., I felt him pick me up.

"Baby, go back to sleep. I'm taking you to bed now," he said. He had taken a pool towel from the bathroom and wrapped me in it and was carrying me inside. He pulled back the covers and gently put me into bed, tucking me in. Getting in on the other side, he held us close with our bodies pressed against each other, feeling the warm, tingling vibrations of one another. "I love you, G." He kissed me goodnight and went to sleep.

At 8:30 a.m., the warm sun was peeking through a small crack in the curtains, summoning me to wake up. I rolled over and put my leg around the Greek. I rubbed my hand on the sheet to warm it up so I could massage his manhood. It got hard very fast. A few minutes later, he rolled on top of me, inserting himself as he did. The Greek was up and ready for more action.

"*Kalimera*, baby," he said lustfully, breathing harder on my neck. "Want to be part of the British Airways mile-high club later?" He giggled as he buried himself inside me.

Not sure if he was kidding, I giggled at the suggestion, causing him to go flaccid. It gave us both a good laugh but left us unsatisfied.

"We're going to have a great life, G," he said as he rolled over, waiting to get hard again. "You know I want a son with you, but I want you for myself for a while." He told me he wanted to get to know everything about me and everything that had happened since we left off. He also wanted to finish his treatment program before bringing kids into the world, which was a grown-up view that I was pleased with.

Later that morning, after several rounds of lovemaking, we checked out of the hotel and said our goodbyes to Bridgette and Leon, who were very much hung over, having stayed up partying with Rick and Alana until the wee hours of the morning. They were checking out and heading to Milan for the Christmas holiday. Sebastian's parents, meanwhile, were staying one more night in Greece to visit with some extended family. They were on their way out of the hotel when we left for the airport.

We had boarded our flight back to London, and right after getting buckled in, the flight attendant came over and asked us if it was true that we had just gotten married. She'd seen it in the news.

"That fast, huh?" was Sebastian reply. He looked over at me as he reclined his seat back before closing his eyes. "Get ready for when it hits, Gina," he said, preparing me to deal with the reaction from his legion of loyal female fans. He turned toward me and raised the armrest, taking a blanket and putting it around our laps. Then he asked me with a snicker, "Mile High" can you give me a hand job?"

Some things change, and some seem to stay the same, I thought. Looking at him with a raised eyebrow, I put the arm rest down. "My tour days are over, my road name is retired, and you can wait till I'm home …and yes, the pun was intended," I said, putting the armrest down to curb his enthusiasm.

After the four-hour flight, we collected our luggage. I had to go through the customs line. Sebastian waited on the other side for me with his driver.

"What happened to the suitcase I bought you?" Sebastian asked as the driver loaded the luggage into the back of the car.

I told Sebastian that it was painful for me to look at it and that I had given the bag to Leon. I said it was like the TV trays at his house that I associated with his ex-wife.

"You really do connect things with people, don't you?" Sebastian stated with an odd look on his face.

"Yes, because I can see the person it's attached to," I replied.

Sebastian paused, taking a moment to observe me. Then he smiled, looked down, and shook his head.

When Sebastian and I arrived home, Melba and Nigel were outside on the property. They started to approach the car as we parked in the driveway. Sebastian opened the door and was greeted by Nigel.

"Bloody hell, ya went off and got yourselves hitched? It's all over the telly. Congratulations, then." Nigel's wife Melba came over to give me a hug as I got out of the car. "We'll leave you to it. Come, Melba, we'll get the skinny later." He and Melba started walking back to their house. They had only gotten a few feet away when Nigel turned around and said, "Bas, your blower has been going all day."

"What's a blower?" I asked, confused

"The phone," Sebastian replied, figuring that everyone in his circle had seen the news by now. "Shall we go turn on the news and see what we did?"

We walked into the house and headed for the bedroom. Sebastian turned to the BBC, and the marriage of Sebastian Roland was breaking news. I asked him how in the hell that information could possibly be known in London; we had just gotten married. Sebastian explained that you can't do anything in Europe and people not know about it. He assumed that the info had circulated at the restaurant and that the hotel had confirmed later that we did in fact get married there. I suggested that Sebastian check his blower's answering machine to see how many calls were waiting. The first message was from Lacey saying she wasn't in shock. The news hadn't hit the States yet, but she'd heard about it from Joe. There was a message from Stan. He was pissed that he'd heard it from Chip, but that reaction was to be expected. Chip left a message saying he'd heard the news from Joe and Andy but didn't believe it and asked Sebastian to call him back.

The best comments were left by Andy and Joe, the guys from Raiders of Doom, who left him an inebriated message.

"Lost the plot, Bas? Gina married your barmy fucking arse?" Andy said, completely wasted.

"They're both mad as a bag of ferrets, I tell ya," Joe said, laughing really hard.

"Neither one is batting on a full wicket," Andy said, laughing at Joe's comment.

"He's a git, Gina!" Joe said, laughing into the phone.

"All right, then, the BBC said it, so cheers, mate," Andy said. He then hung up the phone, though from the sounds of it, it took a few tries to do so.

I had some idea what the guys had said, but Sebastian explained the Americanized version of their banter to me, and I started laughing. Sebastian wanted to save that message because it was funny.

The next message from Stan was erased, however. "Did you lose your mind? You should have told me you were getting married. I would have been prepared to handle the press on this one, Bas."

Sebastian didn't care what Stan had to deal with regarding him or Tin Garden issues; he was paid to deal with it. Sebastian and the guys had grown tired of Stan's BS, and talking about releasing Stan from his management duties. Either way, he would not be touring with them anymore. I stayed out of the band stuff. It was never my place to comment on Stan; he had been the band's manager for several years. He was good at his job, but he was also a tyrant, dubbed a czar by the crew for good reason. He didn't treat people with respect, not even the members of the band he was working for. I always took this position regarding Tin Garden: never give my opinion, never my problem.

After checking messages, Sebastian wanted to pick up where we had left off. We were both exhausted and only had a week to ourselves before Sebastian would move out for rehab and Leon would move in to keep me occupied. Lying in bed, Sebastian said that he would be able to call me every day but that I wouldn't be able to see him for a month, so we needed to clock in some heavy-duty sexy time, which we did. We spoke about starting a family and the names we would call our kids. Sebastian suggested that if we had a boy, he wanted to name him Adonis Richard Roland, taking Sebastian's middle name and his father's first name. If we had a girl, I suggested Dionysus. Sebastian gave me an odd stare and shot that suggestion down, suggesting Rhea Eos Roland instead. Eos was his mother's middle name.

It was getting near dinner time, and I went downstairs to make a stew. As usual, I put his dinner on his tray and brought it to him. Setting the tray over his naked body, I asked, "Can I see if Nigel can take me to Harrods tomorrow to buy some new trays?"

"You and I can do that. Is that what you want for Christmas? TV trays?" he asked with a snicker.

"I already got my Christmas present … it was you," I said seriously.

"Me too, baby. Me too" Sebastian said with a small grin and serious look on his face as he leaned in to kiss me.

After dinner, Sebastian wanted to address something serious. He was concerned that I didn't eat, especially in his presence. I assured him that I did eat and that when I got pregnant, that was not going to be an issue.

"Really, Gina? I want us to have a healthy baby, and I need you to eat in front of me. I have to tell you, G, it really bothers me a lot that I never see you eat," he said, concerned.

I understood where he was coming from. I didn't have a food issue or eating disorder; I just didn't eat much. I ate when I was hungry.

"I never want you to think that you can't eat in front of me, like I would judge you or something. That would be really fucked up." Then he asked if I was a vegetarian. I told him I wasn't. Sebastian asked me to go downstairs and bringing up a plate of what I deemed to be a typical meal. I looked at him like he was crazy but went downstairs to the fridge. I pulled out some cheddar cheese, got some crackers, and cut up some melon and brought it back to the bedroom.

"This is what you eat? That's it?" Sebastian was looking at my plate and had a sad look on his face. "Who shamed you into not eating, Gina? Was it a guy?"

Pondering his question, I knew exactly when my "eating disorder" began. I told Sebastian it was in New York when I was working twelve hours a day, being shamed into not eating bread. I told him that in the theater, it was required to be thin.

Sebastian shook his head. "For ballerinas, maybe. Theater? No, G." He insisted that I could eat all of the bread I wanted, and he would actually be happy about it. "Tomorrow when we go over to Harrods, I'm going to take you to their Parisian tea room and watch you eat some macaroons," he said, laughing.

After he made his bread declaration to me, I asked myself, *If I had been twenty pounds heavier, would he have had interest in me when I met him back in New York? No, he wouldn't have. I saw the girls he dated, thin model types. Food issues? I'm back to that with him again? Macaroons? How about this: get off my ass and go back to rehab, jackass.*

Do They Know It's Christmas?

Sebastian and I left for a shopping excursion at Harrods. I got to pick out new trays, and Sebastian had several packages waiting for him that were wrapped and ready for pickup. Assuming there may be one in there for me, I managed, when he went off to use the restroom, to sneak in another present to put under the tree for Sebastian from Santa: some underwear to take to rehab. We picked out a Harrods hamper full of booze and food for Melba and Nigel, and Sebastian picked out a special toy for David—a children's piano. Sebastian was going to teach him how to play. As we waited for the car to be brought around, Sebastian said that after rehab, he wanted to take me on a proper honeymoon. He asked me where I would like to go. I suggested we go back to New York and stay at the Carlyle, like we did when we first met, but he suggested that someplace like Malta might be more romantic. I thought the most romantic place to go with him was back to the place I had met him, but I did want to revisit Greece sometime soon. Sebastian told me Athens was okay but said I would probably like Santorini better. The car arrived, and packages were spilled into the back seat. With a car full of Santa's gifts, we headed back to Surrey.

I loved spending this time with him. We'd never shopped or done anything like that before. Sebastian's idea of shopping was to make a call to someone and have a garment bag delivered. This was way more fun for me, but I knew this would be a rare experience in our marriage when he expressed his hatred for "shopping for shit."

When we got on the road, he turned to me and said, "I want to take you into the guest room when we get home. I thought about that when you bent over looking at that hamper for Nigel and Melba."

I shot him a smirk and thought to myself, *Oh, old Sebastian, I knew you were in there somewhere. You have come back to me.*

We pulled into the driveway. Sebastian parked the car and said to "leave the crap." He would get it later. He went over to my side of the car, picked me up off the ground with his arm under my legs, and put me over his shoulder caveman style, with me in a playful struggle to get loose.

Sebastian took me in the front door and into the guest bedroom, laying me down backside to the bed. "I want to make love to you the rest of the night," he said, positioning himself on top of me. "I never get tired of you, but you do have a way of wearing me out. That's not a bad thing."

He began breathing hard on my neck as he removed my clothes. Sebastian was growing larger by the moment as I unbuttoned his pants and slid them down. I then assisted him inside of me. Our lovemaking was slow at first, then it picked up pace when he arched his back. Sebastian's long hair was covering his face as he moved back and forth inside of me. The room started getting darker from lack of natural light. It started to rain, and the room was filled with the sounds of heavy drops of water hitting the glass of the old windows and the creaking of the guest bed as we made romantic love.

"Sebastian, I love you so much," I said as he slowed down and positioned his elbows to the side of me. He framed his hands around my face and passionately kissed me.

We lay there for a few hours after making love, and then he rolled over put on his clothes and went out to the car to bring in the "shit" he'd bought at Harrods, putting it under the tree. He came back into the bedroom, rolled in next to me, and asked if I could make some hot tea and then join him in the library.

Getting up, I went to the kitchen preparing tea and sandwiches. I put them on a plate and brought it into the library. Sebastian had just added a log to the fire. I picked up one of the sandwiches I'd made and started eating it in front of him, pleasing him.

He smiled. "G, I want to give you one of your presents now." He went over to the tree, removed a box from the pile, and handed it to me. He then cozied in with his arm around the back of the couch and watched me open it.

I removed the lid. Inside was a piece of paper with a handwritten message. It read, "Gina, I will love you till the other side of time.

Sebastian." It was the most beautiful thing I had ever gotten from him. I kissed and held him. His words were so beautiful.

"I said that to you on our wedding day, and I meant it, G. There is another part to that gift. I'm having my lawyer make it so that you are the one who will be in charge of my publishing rights and music, everything Tin Garden, in case something ever happens to me. You will always be taken care of, and the guys can't take it from you, Gina," he said, holding me.

"Sebastian, I don't want that stuff. I want you," I said, crying at the thought of him leaving.

"I want to protect you. I never did this with my ex. Maybe I knew deep down she couldn't be trusted; I don't know. But I trust you, Gina. I have no doubts about you."

"What you wrote means more to me than anything," I said, looking into his eyes.

"I know, G, and given your reaction to it, I know it's the right thing to do."

I was taken aback by everything he was doing. I was happier with the piece of paper that had his words on it with than anything Tin Garden could ever leave me with, and he knew it.

Sebastian brought me closer to his chest, and we cuddled on the couch. He stroked my hair, telling me about his Christmas traditions with his family, which included everyone coming to his house. It was the most comfortable for everyone, since the large library had plenty of seating for nearly twenty guests. But he confessed that his mother really liked using his kitchen. "It's not the typical Christmas you're probably used to, Gina. *Mitera* likes to do Greek food."

He asked me about my family holiday traditions. I told him that I always went over to my grandparent's house for Polish food at Christmas. He looked at me inquisitively.

"I thought you said you were Irish," he said. I said I was on my father's side of the family, not my mother's side.

It was getting late, and he suggested going to bed before Santa passed us over. I laughed and took my present upstairs, placing it inside the gap in the dresser mirror so I could stare at it every morning.

We were making love into the early hours when we heard a thump downstairs. Sebastian said, "Wait here." There was no way I was going to wait alone. "I'm serious, Gina. Wait here." He put on his pants and bolted down the stairs.

He had been down there for a few minutes when I got dressed and headed downstairs after him, grabbing an umbrella that was by the door. "Sebastian, where are you?" I yelled out as he was walking from the kitchen.

"It's nothing, G. Let's go back to bed," he said, taking the umbrella from my hand and propping it against the wall. I grabbed it when he turned around and took it upstairs with me.

"What do you mean nothing, Sebastian? Someone opened the door," I said, worried that someone was still inside. He assured me that nobody was in the house and the doors were locked. He may have checked, but there was no way I would be sleeping with both eyes closed. I kept that umbrella near the bed.

Christmas morning was dreary. I asked the Greek if he wanted coffee. He rolled over and said, "Yes, baby, that would be awesome."

I went downstairs and pulled the coffee out of the refrigerator. When I opened the coffee can, I saw a set of keys sitting on top of the coffee grounds. Confused by this, I took the coffee can back upstairs to show Sebastian.

"Huh, wonder how that got in there? … Did you make the coffee?" he asked, not fazed by keys in the coffee can.

"No, not yet," I replied, shooting him a strange look. He asked me if I would start the coffee and then grab his wellies from the garage. He was uninterested in the keys. Sebastian wanted to take an early walk on the property down to the lake with our morning cup of joe. I went back downstairs and started the coffee, removing the keys from the can. While the coffee was brewing, I walked to the garage to grab his wellies. Turning on the light in the garage, I found myself staring at a black 1986 Aston Martin Vantage with a huge red bow around it and a giant card on the window that read, "Merry Christmas, Gina, from Father Christmas." I ran back into the house.

"Sebastian!"

He was coming downstairs with a smile plastered on his face. He asked what I was yelling about and if the coffee was ready.

"Are you kidding me with coffee right now, Sebastian?" I said with a huge smile from the shock of what I had seen in the garage.

"Did you find my wellies?" he said, laughing, as we walked to the garage. Sebastian looked inside the window of the new car. "You're in luck, G; Santa got you an automatic transmission."

"Sebastian, this is a really expensive car," I said, looking at him in disbelief.

"Gina, you need a car to get around in. You can't drive a stick shift, and I can't drive you everywhere. When we have kids, we'll get a Rover, and I'll keep this one as an alternate."

I figured out that my present was really a present for him but thought it was cute anyway. We went back inside, grabbed our jackets, and headed down toward the lake with our coffee cups in hand. It was a brisk morning. The air was crisp and fresh with the smell of fresh rain mixed with the smoke from burning logs that was coming from Nigel's place. When we spoke, we saw our breath in the cool mist of the morning. We stepped onto the pebble walkway leading to the lake. Puddles had gathered on the grounds from the rain storm. It was quiet and peaceful on our walk, and we enjoyed our time holding hands and looking out over the property. We took a seat on a bench and remained there in a meditative state as we drank our coffee, saying nothing to each other in words but only in vibrations that were emitting from our hands that were locked together. After an hour of just relaxing, we looked at each other at the same time, knowing we needed to get ready for the family brood that would be coming soon. Walking back to the house, we ran into Nigel, who was taking torn Christmas wrappings to the trash can.

"Father Christmas good to you, then?" Nigel said with a laugh. "His damn reindeer got balls-up on the garage door. I tried telling them not to be so loud." Sebastian started laughing. I figured out it was Nigel who had made the noise last night; he had been put in charge of keeping the car hidden from me.

"Yep, he made it to the house," Sebastian replied, and we both wished him and his family a Happy Christmas.

Sebastian wanted to take the car out of the garage and out for a spin. He was more excited about driving it than I was. We went inside to get the keys, and he backed it out of the garage. He then let me into the driver's seat, which was on the opposite side of what I was used to in the United States. It had been a while since I had driven a car. I hadn't had a car in New York and hadn't needed one. I had forgotten when I got to the end of the driveway that I was on the wrong side of the road. Sebastian asked me to pull the car over; he wanted to drive it back to the house.

We exchanged seats, and he said, "Want to see what it can do?" Then he gunned the shit out of it, tearing ass up the driveway and spinning it out when he got to the top of the drive.

"Okay, Double-O-Seven, I won't be doing that trick," I said, giving him a look like he was crazy.

He laughed and said he wanted to leave it in the driveway to show Rick, knowing it was going to piss him off because he actually wanted one just like it.

"That's great, Sebastian. Merry Christmas," I said with a roll of the eyes and a half-hearted smile. I had only been in the family for a few days and wasn't exactly as excited about pissing off my new brother-in-law as he was.

The Christmas festivities were well underway at Mansion Roland. Everyone, including Nigel and his family, had gathered at our house. The women were all in the kitchen, and the men went outside to look at Sebastian's new toy that he said was mine but wasn't really. The children were playing with their new toys from Santa in the library. The guys came back in, and Sebastian said that Rick wanted to drive my car to Simon's Place, the local watering hole in Working, Surrey. The boys' mother told them not to be gone long, because dinner would be ready soon, but she insisted they take their father with them if they went, knowing her boys would lose track of time in a pub. Nigel, Sebastian, Rick, and Richard piled into my new Christmas present and took off for Simon's.

About an hour later, Athene looked at the clock and noticed the men were not back yet. She suggested that Alana call her husband, and Alana retorted that she was not her husband's keeper. Athene gave her an inquisitive look and stated that maybe she needed to be his keeper. Then he might stay home more with his son. With that comment, I decided I would make the call to Simon. I was looking for the number when the guys came walking in the front door. Athene went up to Sebastian and said something to him in Greek. I turned to Alana and asked what that was all about. She said that we would talk about it later; it wasn't the time. I sensed that Alana was aggravated with the boys' mother, but I was too new to the family to get involved and wouldn't have dared mention anything to Sebastian about it.

Athene started to fix the children's dinner plates, getting them settled at the dining room table, and then asked us girls to fix our own men's plates, having Melba go first, since she was an invited guest, followed by Alana, who kind of plopped Rick's plate down in front of him when he was seated. Rick gave her an odd look. I was the last to go. Athene stood over me and watched as I prepared her baby's plate. "Make sure you get the smudges off, Gina, he won't eat off a dirty plate."

I thought to myself, *This guy will eat whatever the hell you put in front of him, and by the way, Athene, he can eat the shit out of a vagina.* But I didn't mention that to her. I just fixed my guy's plate, took it over, and set it in front of him, giving the king at the head of the table a hug after I did.

Athene looked over to Alana and said, "That's how you cater to your man, Alana. That will keep him at home."

There was no way I was going to get mixed up with that comment. I thought, *It's Christmas. Can we just celebrate the reason for the season, already? Jesus. I mean, really ... Jesus.*

After everyone finished eating and there was much banter back and forth across the table about nothing, I got up and started clearing plates, telling Athene that I would do it alone. I told her to go into the library with everyone, and I would prepare tea and coffee. Melba and Alana opted to stay behind and help me. Athene went off with her boys into the library, and the blah-blah-blah Greek was flowing on the way into the library. Nigel and Richard decided they wanted to go outside to look at the new car again, grabbing the keys on the way out just in case they wanted to take a ride. Opening the refrigerator, I noticed that we were out of milk. Melba went over to her house to get some, leaving time for me and Alana to get caught up.

"What was that all about between you and Athene?" I asked Alana, confused at the exchange earlier with the boys' mother.

"She has her own way, Gina. She thinks Rick chases women because I don't take care of him," she replied, upset.

"When this holiday is over, you and I should sit down and have a conversation, Alana," I said. I wanted to offer what assistance I could. Alana was pleased to finally have a person on her side for a change. I had compassion for Alana; she was isolated. I wasn't sure if that was by her own choosing, but I did want to be a friend to her, because she was my sister-in-law.

Nigel and Richard came back and offered help to Alana and me bring the coffee and tea into the library, where we seated ourselves for the fast and furious gift exchange. In the Rolands' way of doing Christmas, you had to pay attention to hear your name being called, or you could get knocked upside the head with a present—too bad, so sad. Rick and Sebastian got up and started tossing packages to everyone.

"*Mitera*!" Sebastian yelled to his mother, who was talking to Melba and got smacked with a package on the side of the leg. "Rick!" He hit Rick in the crotch with the box, causing him to bend over in pain, and they both laughed like a couple of juvenile delinquents.

"Dad!" Rick yelled, tossing the package behind his back. His dad caught it.

This went on for a few minutes until Sebastian yelled, "Melba." She told him she would take the garden sheers to his rose bushes if he tossed it at her. Everyone was laughing, even the kids, who had a blast with the gift toss. Paper tearing could be heard from all directions in the room, and paper was flying in all corners from everyone opening their gifts. Sebastian had one in his hand from me and asked if I would sit next to him when he opened it.

"Should I wait and open this?" he asked, wondering if it was for public consumption.

"Yeah, you can open it." I replied, knowing it wouldn't offend anyone. He started to take the paper off slowly, looking at me as he removed the lid from the box. Inside was a new silver chain for his jeans, along with a new, black-leather wallet.

"Baby, this is really nice," he said, looking at it and seeing it was personalized. "*Mitera*, look." I'd had a store in Greece emboss the following inside the wallet: Για Ανα ΑΈλληνα θεό μουΟ Αγάπη, G.

Not knowing if it was transcribed correctly, I asked him what it said.

"To my Greek god. Love, G," he replied with a smile. His mother seemed pleased with my selection, stating that it was very thoughtful gift. Sebastian invited me to come into the kitchen for a minute.

"I love my gift," he said, backing me into a corner of the counter and pushing his manhood up against me.

Just as he was thanking me for the gift, Rick walked into the kitchen. "Oh, yeah. Newlyweds. Sorry, kids. I'll call you tomorrow, Bas."

Sebastian turned around to acknowledge him. "Don't call me with Stan bullshit," he said pointedly.

"Back the bus up. We're on break. I know better than that, Bas," Rick replied defensively.

Melba and Nigel were collecting their gifts and kids and heading toward the kitchen door. Sebastian stopped Nigel and asked him to come to the back room. They returned a few minutes later, and Nigel shook Sebastian's hand and gave him a hug. It must have been a Christmas bonus, because he was holding an envelope when he came out, and Sebastian said, "Use it for the family, not the ponies."

Everyone had left, and the house was a mess. I started to get a trash bag to clean up the paper.

"Sit down, G. Let it go. We'll get it tomorrow; I want to relax," Sebastian said, and I took a seat next to him and curled up. "Just think, when we have our own kids, it'll be chaos." He laughed and then reached under the couch and handed me another box to open. "I wanted to give this one to you when we were alone." He had a smile plastered on his face.

The package was wrapped in a London Times newspaper; obviously, he had done that all by himself. Ripping off the paper, I opened the box, and inside staring back at me was my old stage outfit from the "Wait Tour."

"I stole it from wardrobe when Emily wasn't looking. I'd held on to it all of this time, and I wanted you to have it back," he said with the look of the devil in his eyes.

I wasn't sure how I felt about staring at my old stage outfit sitting inside that box. I mean, yeah, it was thoughtful that he stole something and then kept it as a souvenir of our relationship, but he actually bought the thing with Tin Garden funds. I actually hated the damn thing. That outfit was the topic of more arguments, started by him, than I ever bargained for, but it's the thought that counts. Besides, he'd already bought me—I mean, him—a car for Christmas.

Cold Turkey

Sebastian and I spent New Year's Eve at Casa Roland by ourselves. It was a quiet evening at home where we made poor man's pizza by flattening out biscuit dough and putting sauce, cheese, and meat on top. After our pizza, we spent several hours having sex in every room of the house, wanting to see how long we could do it before (a) getting board or (b) running out of steam. It seems *b* prevailed.

Sebastian was going back into rehab on January 2. We were both sad about being apart for the thirty days, but this was a necessary item on his shit-to-do list. His demeanor on New Year's Day was detached. The program was not something he wanted to do; he chose to get sober so we could start our family. A relationship with Sebastian without rehab would not be a long road traveled, and he knew it. He'd been on pills, booze, and cocaine when we met. Later in our relationship, his usage had gotten more excessive than when I had first met him. He hadn't been able to function without substances. The pills brought out the worst in him: irrational behavior, mood swings, and hateful outbursts. He was prescribed opioids as the "medicine" to help him get off of heroin, which he'd begun using shortly after he married Vail. He claimed it was his way of coping with a person who never loved him but used him excessively to boost up her own career and lifestyle. I didn't buy into his explanation for his heroin use for a minute. He had anxiety issues. Vail used him, yes, but I felt it wasn't her narcissism that made him need to use heroin. Bottom line was, Sebastian had an addictive personality. Some people have things they might be addicted to—sugar, gambling, booze, sex, whatever. I'm not judging. Sebastian was heavily addicted to Tuinal, which was destroying his mind and had nearly taken his soul. I wasn't sure what the catalyst was for him hitting his bottom; nobody knew. But he was on the road to recovery, and I was going to support him on each day on his journey.

It was rehab entry day, and Sebastian was packing the last of his things into his suitcase, tossing it with major attitude down the steps.

It landed by the door. He was distant and in a bitter mood. I assured him that the time would fly by and that I was using this time for myself to go back to New York with Leon and get my things from the apartment before Leon left Europe to go back home. He liked the idea that Leon was staying on with me for a few weeks. It made it easier, he said, to go back into rehab. He wouldn't worry about me as much with Leon at the house. Before getting in the car, he wanted one last romp, because as he put it, being dry for thirty days was more than he could handle with no conjugal visits. Sebastian was being dramatic, but we had a good roll in the hay anyway before driving to the rehab facility about forty minutes away in London.

Once we arrived, he started tearing up. I knew this was hard on him. He was not only admitting he had a drug problem but he also had to face it head on and alone. We walked into the facility together and were met by an intake person, who took his suitcase for inspection. My heart sank when I was told by a staff member that I wouldn't be able to see him for at least thirty days. There was a family meeting day that would be taking place around that time, with Sebastian deciding who would be in attendance at that meeting. Just because we were married did not give me access to the meeting or him while he was going through treatment. He could walk out of his own free will at any time, but it was suggested that he needed to finish the program. After he was signed in, we hugged for a good five minutes until someone came and took him away. At the glass door, he turned around with tears in his eyes and said, "I'm doing this for us. I love you, G." Then he walked into the facility.

I sat there for a few minutes just looking into the room they'd taken him to and started crying. I was told by the intake person that it would be better for me if I went home instead of torturing myself and that he would be fine. I was aggravated at the coldness of the intake person and thought that if she had any idea what I had been through with him, she would have let me sit there for a few more minutes. The intake person looked at me with a cold stare and said, "We'll have Mr. Roland call you later." And then I was dismissed. I was in tears as I left the facility. I had a feeling leaving him there like I was leaving a puppy at the shelter—sadness.

I walked to the car and made the drive back to Surrey. When I pulled up the drive, Nigel was tending the grounds. He saw that I had been crying and came over to ask if I had taken Sebastian to London. Everyone in his circle used the phrase *going to London*, like he was going away to summer camp. Even his family did this. I told Nigel that yes, I had taken Sebastian to "rehab." Nigel was caught off-guard by me saying the word *rehab*. I told Nigel that everyone needed to stop walking around on eggshells and label his problem what it was: a problem with pills and drugs that required rehab.

I was a bit frustrated with Nigel's denial of his employer's drug problem and went inside the house. Leon was due to come into Heathrow soon, and I made a call to invite Alana to come over and join us. Alana agreed to come over, because Rick was going into London for the afternoon and was taking David with him to visit Joe from Raiders of Doom. She had taken a pass on going with him—strike one. This was really part of Alana's problem with Rick. She had removed herself so much out of Rick's life that it made sense to me why he sought extracurricular activities. It really was none of my business, but I really wanted to help this girl out with just a little info about being married to a music man.

Alana walked into the house where I was in the kitchen making sandwiches, knowing that Leon would be hungry. Since Alana didn't cook—strike two—I figured she hadn't eaten either. When I told her I had sandwiches ready, Alana replied, "Great, I haven't eaten all day."

Alana and I were getting food on the table when Leon yelled from the front door, "Damn, girl, this is one huge estate. Took ten minutes just to go up the driveway." He had the driver bring in his suitcase and set it in the foyer.

I ran over to the door to greet him and told him that Alana had stopped over for a visit and was in the kitchen. I leaned in close to his ear. "We may need to stage an intervention," I said. He rolled his eyes at me, asking what the hell had happened over Christmas.

We sat down, and Leon began telling Alana and me all about

Milan and Christmas with Bridgette's family. He told us how he went to Venice and how we would really love the place, because it was really different than other places he had seen, especially when it rains. The entire city floods. He was still mad at me for missing Christmas with him, but Bridgette's family understood when they turned on the television the day after the wedding why Bridgette had left so abruptly and why I was missing out on their holiday. Leon was shocked that the wedding of Sebastian Roland actually made it on the Italian news.

Leon settled into his chair and grabbed a sandwich and then asked if I had any liquor in the house, since Sebastian was dry now. I got up and went into the library to make him a Manhattan, leaving him to talk with Alana. I overheard them talking as I came back into the kitchen, setting his drink down.

He asked, "Did you take SoBo to rehab?" Alana seemed shocked by Leon's question.

"Yes, he's in rehab, and he will be there for thirty days, unless he needs more time," I stated casually. I had run out of bandwidth to handle the denial of everyone in Sebastian's circle, especially his family, about his big issue. I told Alana about how Sebastian's pill problem got excessive on the road and how it had gotten out of hand toward the end of the tour. I told her that if his parents had seen him during that time, they would be calling his stay in London *rehab* also. I then told Alana what he'd done to me when he was messed up on pills, and Leon confirmed Sebastian's abusive behavior. Leon had been there; he'd seen what was going on. We were all using substances, but Sebastian's usage was just more excessive than anyone else on that tour. I was proud of Sebastian for taking control of his issues and going back into rehab, but it was an intense program, because he had previously been addicted to heroin. Alana was actually shocked to hear that Sebastian was addicted to pills, and I was more shocked that Alana didn't even know. Alana had assumed that Sebastian was just really depressed in his marriage.

We were still discussing Sebastian's drug issues when Leon, wanting to change the subject, turned to Alana and asked how Rick was. Alana, looking down at her sandwich, stated casually that he was off in London with the Raiders of Doom guys and had taken David with him.

"Rick took your son out with those cats?" Leon asked, surprised.

Alana seemed taken aback at Leon's reaction; she hadn't realized that Leon knew them well. Leon started to recount a tour play-by-play for Alana as I quickly withdrew from their discussion.

"Those Raider guys are a hot damn mess. Gina will tell you; she knows."

Alana looked over at me with tears forming in her eyes, and I turned to Leon, asking him to back off of the conversation.

"I know Rick cheats on me; I've known it for a really long time. That's where he is today, at his lover's house. He's not with Joe or Andy," Alana said as she started crying. "David is at his grandparents' house tonight, and Rick is seeing someone, Gina." Alana was now crying her eyes out.

Leon and I sat there in disbelief and shock. I asked her if she knew who the person was he was seeing, and she said she didn't know the name. I asked her if Rick stayed out all night or came home. Alana told us that he usually came home around 1:00 a.m. or so. Leon, taking all of this in, hesitated for a minute and then leaned in toward me and said that it was Emily. I looked at him and shook my head no way.

"You say this person lives in London?" Leon asked Alana pointedly.

"Yes, that I know for sure, because I check the millage on his car. He drives to London," Alana replied.

"It's Emily, girl," Leon stated, looking at me, certain it was her.

"No way, Leon. She was on our bus for the tour," I stated.

"She moved off when Sebastian came aboard," Leon replied matter-of-factly.

"But she moved back on when Rick came aboard in Memphis … Oh, shit," I said, seeing it play out as if I were looking back in time. On the tour, Emily had moved off our bus when Sebastian moved on full time. Rick decided he would take over our bus one evening in Memphis, and that's when Emily moved back on. I told Alana that I'd never seen them together, but Leon stated sarcastically that he had. The light of truth shined on me when I realized that Emily and her crew had resided in a hotel separate from the band's residence at the Carlyle and that Rick never partied with us in New York. Rick was one sneaky bastard.

"Who's Emily?" Alana asked.

"The stitch bitch," Leon retorted. The three of us sat there looking at each other in silence. I thought it best for Alana to wait until Rick returned home so she could confront him directly with what Leon had said. Alana was angry, and she asked Leon if he had Emily's number. She wanted to make the call to see if Rick was there. I got up from the table. I wanted no part of this drama, but I felt I was being implicated in it no matter what happened. I had made a promise to Rick never to discuss his personal business with his wife, and I had every intention of keeping it.

While Leon was getting Emily's number, I asked Alana if Sebastian knew about Rick's current extramarital affair. "If Leon knows, your Sebastian does too," Alana replied, aggravated.

Leon had his phone book in hand, and he wrote down Emily's phone number on a piece of paper. Leon was supposed to interview for a fashion-show gig with Emily, but he was currently rethinking that due to the new information spilling onto my kitchen table.

I had found out in Athens that these guys were getting sucked off in their dressing rooms, but my God, I would've never thought Rick was having an affair with Emily. This information was shedding light on Athene's attitude toward Alana at Christmas. She knew what was going on with her boy.

I suggested to Alana that maybe Rick was bored and that she might spice things up with him, do things for him, like learn how to cook, so he wouldn't go out and look for someone like Emily, who was nothing more than a party girl with a cool job. Alana seemed pissed off at my suggestion. I couldn't understand why Alana had this attitude and thought she'd kind of brought this affair on herself. Guys who cheat are assholes, no doubt, but if you're not taking care of your man, he will go off the reservation and get attention from whoever is available to give it. Kids or no kids, this is a fact of life with men, and Alana needed to do whatever had to be done to keep her man happy and at home. Learning Greek was not going to make her issues go away; it had only confirmed for her what she already knew he was doing on the road: having sex with other women.

I told Alana to forget the language courses; she needed to take a cooking class and learn how to cook for her child and her husband instead of having Rick cook meals for her kid. I thought, *Jesus, girl, get with the program.* I was losing sympathy for her by the minute, even though I didn't agree with how Rick handled his affairs. Communication was always a better choice than sticking your dick into the stitch bitch any day of the week.

Alana thanked Leon for the intel but wasn't sure what she was going to do or say to Rick or how she was going to confront him. Alana did tell us that she had no intention of implicating Leon or me in her acquisition of the information she was going to present to Rick, but I couldn't see how we couldn't be implicated; we both knew her. Alana took Emily's number and headed home.

"The Roland boys are seriously twisted up with it. I wish you would've waited to marry his fucked-up ass. You caught your man in the act, too, girl," Leon said, aggravated at me for getting married too soon. "I ain't doing round two of this shit. That man breaks your heart again, and I will hire someone to kick his ass. I'm being real with you, Gina. Dead real." Leon was pissed off at the Roland boy drama. It was old news; it was just that it was only coming to the surface now, which I pointed out to him. Leon and I had never spoken about what happened on the tour, mainly because it was painful for me. After I left, I wanted to move forward, not relive it.

After Alana left, I took Leon by the hand and showed him where his room was. He put his suitcase in the guest bedroom and said that we would have a pj night and popcorn and that he would probably fall asleep in my bed, as long as I changed the sheets from my man. He didn't want to sleep on top of Sebastian's nastiness.

"G, you know I can't be rolling around in Roland mess." Leon laughed. "You Roland bitches are a hot damn mess!" he said, laughing down the hallway.

I was laughing at his comment too when I tripped on the rug

in the hall and fell to the ground. Leon turned around and saw me laughing at myself. "I'm happy you're here; obviously, I need help," I said, laughing because I wasn't even able to stand on my own two feet. We both had a really good laugh at my expense. I was happy to have my best friend back.

After Leon got settled in, I took him outside to see the present Sebastian had bought me for Christmas. Leon wasn't easily impressed by the car, because neither one of us drove. Being chauffeured was always a better way to go than driving in our book. Leon, looking at it, stated that it was an expensive gift. I sneered and told Leon that it had actually been a gift from Sebastian to himself.

"I knew it was. Don't know why you bothered me with this," Leon replied. He was dialed in.

We made our popcorn, and as the smell the butter went through the house, we took the huge bowl upstairs to watch a movie. Sebastian had a huge collection of movies, and we decided on *The Godfather*. A *familia* vehicle seemed fitting after Leon's stay with Bridgette in Italy.

We settled into my bed with all of the pillows piled up at our backs and began deciding on who was going to do which character in the movie dialogue. I wanted to do the Godfather and Clemenza, but Leon said that he was doing Clemenza and Michael Corleone and I could do the part of Sonny. I agreed to my new role, because Leon was a guest.

An hour into the movie, as we were getting ready to do the infamous cannoli line, the phone rang. We let out a disappointed "noooo," pausing the movie so he (we) could do it later. We had waited an hour just to say "leave the gun …" Sebastian was calling to ask me if Leon had arrived; I was on the phone with a huge smile on my face.

"Were just watching a movie," I said, and Sebastian paused and asked if I would put Leon on the phone. I didn't even look at him, I just handed him the phone.

Leon took the phone receiver and rolled his eyes. "What does he think? Some other man is up in this house? Lord, he is a mess with it." He took the phone from my hand. "Hello, SoBo," Leon said, laughing to Sebastian on the phone. "Uh huh, well, I'm in bed with your hot wife watching a movie. Probably going to sleep with her, too. Keep that thought in your mind when you go to bed tonight. Bye-bye, now." Leon laughed and handed the phone back to me.

I rolled my eyes at Leon, taking the phone back. Sebastian, in a distant tone, asked me if I was having a good time. I assured him that we were watching a movie and were staying in for the evening. What I really wanted to know was how day one of rehab was going.

"It's rehab. It sucks," Sebastian said. I knew he was upset because he wasn't at home and not because of Leon's comment.

I got up out of bed, took the phone, and walked downstairs to the guest bedroom. I was sat on the bed telling him how much I missed him and how I looked forward to his calls. He started perking up and began making jokes, asking me if Leon was going to sleep in his bed. I told him yes, to watch a movie. Sebastian told me that he was the one who he wanted to be in bed with me, but I suggested that it was best not to torture himself with that idea.

After a few minutes of rehab talk, he asked me if I would get him off over the phone, saying stuff to him like he was my Greek god and I needed it right now—that nonsense. After a few minutes of listening to the sounds of his hand on his piston whacking himself off, he was nearly ready to rise to his own occasion.

"Baby, I'm coming," he said. This was followed by a series of ahs and ohs. I pulled the phone receiver away from my ear so as not to hear that. The only thing I wanted to hear in my ear was Leon doing the cannoli line.

I went back upstairs, and Leon and I finished watching the movie. Then we talked about going to Harrods in the morning and taking in some of the sights in London. Leon told me he would give Emily a call to back out of the fashion gig in light of the new Rick information, but after we spoke about it, we decided there was no need for him to do that. Business comes first. Leon was trying to get established in the fashion world, and she was his ticket in. He told me that he was going to come clean with Emily about Rick and his involvement in spilling her business with Alana. I thought it was a good idea to tell Emily the truth about what Alana knew at this point, but I was insistent with Leon that I could have nothing to do with Leon's conversation with her. Leon agreed, but he still took the position that he needed to wipe his slate clean with Emily.

West End Girls

The following morning, I was making breakfast when Leon came into the kitchen and sat down. Leon looked subdued when he took his seat at the table, putting bacon and eggs on his plate and shaking his head in disbelief.

"They're sleeping together; it's been going on since the tour ended. She's in love with him," Leon said as he related how his conversation with Emily had gone. He said that Rick had told her that he was asking Alana for a divorce so they could be together. I paused in disgust and told Leon that I had heard enough but that I didn't believe it.

After breakfast, we headed out of the house for our drive into London for the day. Nigel was tending to the grounds. I walked Leon over and introduced him to Nigel before heading down the driveway, taking the roads that led to London. This was only my second time driving to Harrods. I was directionally challenged, but not when there was a fabulous store I needed to get to. I seemed to be able to navigate that with no problem. We arrived at Harrods and decided to have a spot of lunch before shopping, which we did for a good three hours. After we spent a better part of the day shopping, Leon suggested that we get the car and drive by the Queen's pad. When we got near Buckingham Palace, Leon put his arm out the window and did a proper wave.

"I've always wanted to do that. She ain't the only queen up in this town, girl," he said, and we both laughed.

Heading back to the house, I told Leon what Sebastian had said about wanting to add me to all of his bank accounts and give me the publishing rights to all his music.

"Publishing rights? He can only do that if his name is the one on the writing credits," Leon stated, confused. "We need to look at one of their albums and see who is credited for writing their lyrics, but I think you'd get that anyway when he dies. Yoko did. Shit, and she be livin' too." He sat back in his seat in disbelief.

When we got back to the house, Leon tore ass through the front door and went straight into the music library to scan through the albums that were lining the wall. "This man don't put nothing in order ... Didn't you work in a library? You need to get his mess together so you can find shit," he said, frustrated with the albums not being in alphabetical order. Finally, he located a Tin Garden album and tore out the inner sleeve, throwing the cover to the floor. He surveyed the printed lyrics and credits with a critical eye. "Well, he is the only one credited for the lyrics on their last album, so I guess he was right about that." He picked up the album jacket from the floor, placing it on top of the others sitting on the shelf, and apologized to me for being suspicious. I understood why Leon was being critical. Sebastian needed to earn Leon's trust back; it had been broken.

New York State of Mind

Leon had been in London for a few weeks when he decided that he needed to get back to New York. It had always been my plan to go back with him to get my things. Sebastian was still in rehab, and I was speaking with him every night, but he was getting restless in the facility. Treatment was going well, but he had told me that he wanted to come home and start a family. It was rough for him being there, but it was a necessity for him to be clean and sober before we could think about starting a family. I would use the time while he was going through treatment to go back to New York with Leon so I could pack my things, pay my rent for the year, and ship back whatever I needed to. When I left for Greece, I'd had no idea that I would be getting married and staying in Europe. I wanted to make things easier for Leon to handle in my absence. We had just moved into the place, and I didn't want to leave Leon high and dry carrying the rent payment alone.

Leon and I had always wanted to fly on the Concorde. It was a relatively new concept in conventional flying that allowed passengers to get to New York in a matter of a few hours. I booked the thousand-dollar seats, and we headed for London Heathrow the following day.

Upon arriving at Heathrow, we boarded the British Concorde flight back to JFK. Taking off was scary as hell. The plane flew at a surprising supersonic speed. When we reached their cruising altitude, Leon asked the flight attendant to bring him two double Manhattans and sick bag. He told me that the takeoff had made him edgy. I was seated next to the window. Looking out, I could see the curvature of the earth and thought about how amazing that was. Leon wanted no part of it. He got up and went to the restroom with his sick bag. After a few minutes, he emerged from the bathroom and stated that he was better. He slammed his two cocktails and ordered two more.

I put my hand to the window and found that it was hot to the touch, probably due to the speed and altitude at which the plane flew. I looked over at Leon. "Feel this," I said. He put his hand to the window, giving me a peculiar look, and asked me not to utter the words *Greek* or *god* while on the flight. Then he got up and went back to the bathroom. Leon did not enjoy his Concorde experience. I thought it was pretty fabulous.

The flight from London to New York was only three and half hours. I thought it was money well spent. When we landed at JFK, Leon stated that he would never fly on the Concorde again. He was happy to be on the ground. Once we went through customs, we hailed a cab back to our apartment in midtown. It was good to be back home for the both of us. I'd missed New York but not the snow we saw piled alongside Interstate 495 as we headed into the city.

The cab pulled up to our apartment. Taking the elevator to the fifth floor, we set our bags down at the door. Leon's nerves were shot from the flight, and he said that he was going to go lay on the sofa, which he did, going straight to sleep. While Leon was sleeping, I decided to give Lex a call to find out how his holidays were and to let him know that I had gotten married while in Greece. With Lex, it was best he heard the news from my mouth directly. I went to my room and placed the call.

"Lex, it's Gina. How are you?"

"Gina, darling, shall I assume that the post office lost my engraved invitation and that it will be arriving after the holidays?" Lex said with a disappointed tone.

I told Lex what had happened in Greece, that I had gotten married.

"Imagine waking up on Christmas morning, getting your coffee ready, going to the door to fetch your newspaper, and seeing you and Sebastian Roland splashed across Page Six. It read like a tragic, teenage after-school special." He paused. "I sent Carl to the market on Jesus's birthday to pick up several copies, just to see if Santa Clause had left that for me alone or for all of Manhattan," Lex said in a snarky, pointed tone, thinking he had purposefully not been invited my wedding.

I got Lex to calm down. He received my news with shock and surprise, and we arranged to meet for coffee in midtown at a local bistro. He wanted to hear the story in person.

I headed out to a corner bistro by my apartment. When I walked in, Stan was seated alone in a corner, fumbling through a newspaper. When I slowly approached the table, he looked up.

"Mrs. Roland? This is more than my brain can process right now. Of all the people you could have chosen, why him, Gina? Sit. Tell me everything," Lex said as he shook his head, still in disbelief.

I replayed the events in Greece for Lex, finally getting him to calm down his theatrics. Lex was still in shock. He said he had been concerned over the last few weeks about how to approach me about a project he was working on, suggesting that he must have manifested my marriage to Sebastian, because it actually involved Tin Garden.

"I'm turning Lei Dorme into a rock opera. I was on the verge of asking you how you felt about me reaching out to them before you left for Greece, but obviously now I can stop worrying," Lex said, relieved. I was moved by his kindness in taking my feelings into consideration before asking them, because he didn't need to.

"Did you reach out to Stan yet?" I asked.

"No, I haven't," Lex replied.

"The band's on break; it might be a good time. When Sebastian gets out of rehab, he'll have something to do," I said with a laugh.

"He's in rehab? You know he's been to that rodeo before, right?" Lex said as if I didn't know he had done a stint in rehab.

"He's changed. You wouldn't even recognize him now, Lex," I said, wanting desperately to change the subject. Lex told me that he had to find a suitable rock band to work with, and Tin Garden was his first choice for obvious reasons. Lex was more relaxed and ready to make the necessary calls to Stan to get the ball rolling.

I was happy to catch up with Lex, knowing that we would probably be seeing each other soon if he was able to convince Stan and Tin Garden to move into talks about the production he was working on and the direction he wanted to take the opera. We left the bistro, and I headed back to my apartment.

Headed Back to London

I had been in New York for over a week and had just come back from a visit with Bridgette at the old Christopher Street apartment. Leon was on the phone when I walked in.

"Cool, I'll probably stay with Gina for a few days. Thanks, Em," Leon said as he hung up the phone. He turned to me. "I got that fashion gig in London with Emily!"

"Leon, that's great. I'm so happy for you," I said as I hugged him. Fashion was what Leon had always wanted to do and where he belonged. He had an eye for style that was right on point. Emily was very connected in that world. She also appeared to be very connected to my brother-in-law's penis, something I actually wanted to have a conversation with Sebastian about after his rehab.

"Em said I could stay on with her in London after she gets back from Paris. Do you think Rick will come over for a visit when I'm there?" Leon said, laughing.

"That would actually freak him out if he saw you," I replied,

"Oh, you ain't lying. Do you think Rick will leave his wife?" Leon asked.

"No way," I replied, knowing what I did about Rick. He was a sneaky cheater, but he was devoted to his son. Emily was convenient for him on tour, and it appeared they were still carrying on their post-tour romp at her place in London. My best guess was that the affair would fizzle out once Alana confronted him about it.

I was ready to leave New York, and I placed a call to Nigel to see if he could pick me up at the airport in London when I landed. I tried to get Leon to fly back with me, but he needed to tie up loose ends in New York before heading back. I gathered my things and left the apartment, telling Leon I would see him in a few weeks. I knew I was going home to an empty house, but I felt compelled to be closer to my new husband—and home. It felt right to go back.

I landed at Heathrow, and Nigel was there to pick me up in the new car. Nigel couldn't wait to have an excuse to drive it. I told Nigel it was good to be home, though I found it odd calling England home. With some help from the embassy and my new in-laws, it would be, otherwise I would be going back to the States as an exile every three months.

Nigel took my bags and asked if I really wanted to drive my car. I let him drive it back to the house. Looking over at Nigel, I couldn't figure out how driving a car on the wrong side of the road could bring so much happiness. It's a guy thing that I'll never be able to understand.

Back at the house, Nigel brought in my bags, and I checked the messages. Sebastian had called earlier saying he would try back in an hour. I looked at the clock. Just as his message was finishing, the phone rang.

"Hey, baby, how was New York?" Sebastian asked.

"Good, but I'm happy to be home. I miss you," I replied,

"I miss you too. I called because I have my meeting tomorrow at five o'clock. Can you make it?" Sebastian asked.

"Sure, I can't wait to see you. How are you doing?" I asked.

"I'm good, but I'm ready to come home," he said.

"Do you think things are better for you?"

"I have good days and bad days," Sebastian replied.

"What can I do to help with the bad days?"

"I guess we'll see about that tomorrow, G."

"I admire you for wanting to be well, Sebastian."

"See you tomorrow, G," Sebastian said before hanging up the phone.

After our call, I unpacked my suitcase and started doing laundry. I was preoccupied and wanted to keep busy. My mind was racing with thoughts of how I was going to handle seeing Sebastian. It had been nearly a month, and seeing him again with a counselor in rehab felt odd. I was experiencing a variety of emotions, ranging from fear and anxiety to relief. I had never been through something like this with anyone. It was unknown territory for me.

Running to Stand Still

I arrived at the treatment facility at 4:45 p.m., a few minutes early. I was greeted by Sebastian's counselor, Michael, who lead me to an office and gave me the drill down of how the conversation would be structured during the meeting. Michael informed me that Sebastian had written a letter. This was his way of expressing his transgressions and taking ownership of his role in the hurt he'd caused me and the pain he inflicted on himself with his drug use.

"If Sebastian says 'I'm in here for you,' remind him that he is only in treatment for himself. Sebastian being in treatment may have saved your relationship with him, however it's not the reason he's here," Michael told me.

"Why is he in here, then?" I asked, confused.

"Sebastian is in here to take care of his own physical and mental health. That is the most important thing for him in his sobriety," Michael said in a pointed tone. "Here is how the day will move forward: If Sebastian becomes emotional—and I suspect he will—you need to respond to him in a calm and firm manner, but always let him finish what he needs to say to you. I will move the conversation in a more constructive direction if he becomes irritated."

"Why would he become irritated?" I asked, confused.

"He's working out some difficult issues; be aware of that. The completion of rehab is a very emotional experience for the patient. There is a sense of victory for finishing treatment but a strong sense of fear of relapsing after leaving treatment. It can be overwhelming to his psyche," Michael stated firmly.

"I had no idea what to expect when I came. I'm new to this. He put me through a ton of stuff when he was messed up on pills," I replied sternly.

"It's important to understand that when you see Sebastian, there will be a rush of emotions. It's been almost a month since you've seen him. It's important for you and him to express feelings of joy, not hurt.

It might be difficult for him to express his *own* frustrations while he's sober. Overwhelming him with accusations of things he did in the past will only create an unsafe space for him to be open with you. Do you understand this?" Michael asked.

"So, basically what you are saying is, don't bring up the past, and if he is frustrated with me, roll over?" I asked matter-of-factly.

"Not at all, if he says something you don't like, you need to let him finish what he needs to say. He may struggle to communicate frustrations while he is sober. These things may have nothing to do with you. I know some of what frustrates him—the band, his manager, his record label, staying on top of the music charts, his ex-wife, his desire to be respected over being loved, his desire to stay faithful to you when he tours. He knows if he commits a transgression, it's over." Michael stated, and I was over Michael's last comment.

"What do you mean 'his desire to stay faithful to me when he tours'? I know he has done things, but if he goes outside of us again, it is over," I stated pointedly.

"Creating a safe space for that discussion and letting him explain why being faithful is important to him first is what I suggest to you both. Sebastian is dealing with psychological issues of rejection, not being understood, and depression that are deeply rooted in his psyche. His attempts to cope with those issues led him to substance abuse; that was the only way he thought to handle them. I'm not here to judge him but to teach him how to deal with his issues without substances," Michael explained.

I sat there dumbfounded. "I had no idea he was dealing with all of these psychological issues," I said in disbelief.

"Sebastian told me in session that he feels that you are both spiritually connected, but you don't really know him outside of his stage persona, because as he put it, you never put in the time to get to know him. I'm not saying this to hurt you, but it may come up in our meeting today. I want you to be prepared," Michael said, looking at me directly.

"I love him. I don't give a damn about his stage persona," I replied defensively.

"Then let him explain to you what he feels constructively. I will lead you through the conversation. But allow me to say this respectfully: you didn't know he was dealing with psychological issues, did you? How can you say that you really know him, Gina?" Michael said.

I was starting to feel like I didn't know Sebastian at all. "Oh my God" I said, looking down at the floor as tears began to stream down my face. I had no idea what I was going to say or what I was getting ready to face. I was crying, but I had to collect myself before Michael would agree to get him. Once I dried up my tears, Michael told me to wait in his office and left the room, first turning back to look at me with empathy before leaving to get Sebastian.

I sat in the office chair looking at the photo of Michael's children on his desk. I was numb and confused and felt like I had driven Sebastian to the excessive drug use on the tour. This new information about his inner demons was more than I was able to understand. Staring at the photo on the desk, I wondered if Sebastian and I would ever have children of our own. I thought Michael was right in his assessment; I didn't know him.

Michael and a very subdued Sebastian entered the room. Sebastian came over and gave me a lighthearted hug and a kiss on the check. He was visibly nervous and seemed like he wanted to be anywhere but in that office. Michael took his seat next to Sebastian, who sat on the sofa. I took a seat in a chair in front of them. Sebastian had a piece of paper in his trembling hands. In his eyes, he looked locked, loaded, and ready to fire in my direction by now, but he was a bit nervous with his body language. Michael started the meeting by saying that Sebastian had written a letter that he would like to read out loud. Then he turned it over to Sebastian, who began to read.

Gina,

First I want to say to you how much I love you. You're everything in this world to me that is love, and light where there has been darkness because of

my substance abuse. You're the only girl who doesn't want, or expect anything from me but my love.
He paused here as he started getting frustrated and then continued.

But you don't know me, Gina. All I ever wanted from you was for to know who I am. I would rather have your respect than the love that you offer me.

I know that I have done things in the past when I was fucked up and done other things I knew were wrong. You fell in love with me a little too quickly, by the way, but I took into consideration your age. Knowingly, I took advantage of it, and I admit it. It was wrong of me to do it.

We had an instant connection when we met, but I always thought we would be a short-term tour fling. I would go back home, and you'd go back to New York when it was over. I did try to drive you out of my life many times, to make my life easier. I say this not to hurt you but to be honest with you.

But we progressed, and I started to fall in love with you. It was when you told me you wanted a son that I actually fell in love with you, Gina.

As more time passed, I got pissed off that you never took time to get to know me. I wondered later if you were in love with me or the amped-up stage version of Sebastian. You never looked beyond the Greek god. I hate it when you call me Bas. That name came before you, and when you say it, I know it's to get a reaction out of me. That pisses me off; it shows a lack of respect for me.

I love you, Gina, and the only thing I ever expected from you was your respect of me, not the rock star version of Sebastian you seem to have fallen in love with. I will say, calling me your Greek god still turns me on, and you call still call me that. But next time you say it, I hope it's out of respect for and understanding of me and not because I'm your cock-rocker husband.

I'm sorry for everything I put you through with my addiction. My intention at the video shoot was never to hurt you; it was only to piss you off enough that you would see how much you had hurt me and wake the fuck up. I always thought you were in love with my dick and not me. When you left the tour, I realized how much you did care for me to do what you did. I did push you to leave, but I never intended to destroy us.

I love you,

Sebastian

Sitting there taking in what he said, I was speechless. For the first time in my life, I had nothing to say, not even a witty comeback to slap him with. Looking over at Michael, I had tears streaming down my face. I was numb, and all I wanted to do was get out of there, but I didn't. I waited for permission to speak. Michael turned to me and asked if I had anything I would like to say to Sebastian.

"I had no idea you felt this way. I do respect you, but you're right Sebastian. I can't sit here and deny anything you said. I had no idea this was in your heart or head; you never told me," I said softly, crying.

"I wanted you to figure it out. I wanted you to be authentic, not become someone I wanted you to be for me. Do you get that?" Sebastian replied pointedly.

"I don't have anything to say, Sebastian, except I love you, and now I am afraid to say that to you at all," I said defensively.

"Don't be afraid, Gina. I just want you to love me, not the rock star," Sebastian replied.

"I do love you, Sebastian. I've never been impressed by your stage persona; you know that," I stated firmly.

"Do I, Gina? Do I know that? No, you think you know me, but you don't, G," Sebastian replied in a stern tone.

"You're right, Sebastian. You never told me what demons you were dealing with. How could I have known? You never tell me anything," I replied with a bit of an attitude.

Michael interrupted our conversation and asked me to take a calmer stance.

"I thought you used the pills to get off heroin, which, by the way, made you mean. Now I'm finding out you have other issues, I don't know what to say," I stated with an upward, aggravated inflection in my voice.

"Say that we'll get through this," Sebastian said somberly.

Michael paused the meeting and asked me to step outside. It was getting emotional, and Michael stated he would come and get me if Sebastian was willing to continue.

I was angry as I got up from the chair. I felt like I was the one being attacked in this mess. Sebastian had brought his hands to his head, pulling his hair back from his face. He leaned back into the couch with tears in his eyes. I looked over at him with tears streaming down my face. He wouldn't even look at me when I left the office. I was raw from what he said and bawling my eyes out, because I had no idea if Sebastian wanted a divorce or what the hell was going to happen next. He'd just told me that I didn't know him. I didn't know what to think.

Michael came outside about thirty minutes later to speak to me, saying that Sebastian wanted to see me. Michael thought the meeting had gone in a positive direction, because Sebastian had gotten to lay all his cards out on the table without judgment and ridicule. That was the first time in his life he'd been able to do that. Sebastian was feeling free and liberated, and that was all that mattered as far as Michael was concerned.

I went back inside and took the seat facing Sebastian. He, by now, seemed more relaxed, but I was on pins and needles. I had no idea what to expect next.

"Gina, I'm sorry if what I said hurt. You know I love you, right?" Sebastian asked.

"Sebastian, I don't know what to say. I really don't. I'm not mad; I just don't want to upset you. I want you to be better," I replied, upset.

"Gina, I know you love me; I have never doubted that. I just want you to know me on the inside, baby; that's all," Sebastian replied.

"I'm starting to understand you, Sebastian, and I want you to come home," I replied, crying.

"I'm coming home today," Sebastian said with a smile.

I got up from my chair, went over to the couch, and fell into his lap, crying really hard. We were both holding each other. We'd had a major breakthrough in our relationship. This was communication. Things that had bothered me for months about his nonverbal and dismissive behavior I now started to understand. Holding on to him, I made a silent prayer for anyone who would have to go through treatment alone. *God, give them peace and guide their souls to light and away from the darkness.*

I waited in Michael's office as Sebastian went to collect his things before being discharged. I thanked Michael for all that he had done to help Sebastian. He told me that it was Sebastian who had done the work; he was only there to help guide him. Sebastian had fought his own demons. He also said that he was proud of me for sitting there and taking in the things Sebastian needed to say, and he hoped that it would continue when we got home and started our lives together.

Most people don't start their marriages out with rehab; maybe some do, but it's not the norm. I felt at that moment that I was married to a man I didn't even know, and I was scared to say anything to at this point. I decided to let Sebastian take the lead on everything, walking on his eggshells, if you will. I was willing to do whatever it took to make sure he stayed off drugs.

Sebastian came into the office with his suitcase, and he and Michael went over his appointment schedule. Sebastian would come in once a week for the next six months. Sebastian got up and shook Michael's hand, and then he and I left the office and headed to the car. I handed Sebastian the keys, knowing he wanted to drive.

We started the drive back to Surrey. The car was filled with an awkward silence—that was, until he asked me how Leon was doing. I told him about the gig with Emily, but decided not to bring up any of the other Emily stories that I knew about. It wasn't the right time to dig down on Rick. It might stress him out. I told Sebastian that Leon was coming back to England the following week and asked if it would be okay if Leon stayed at the house for a week until Emily got back from Paris.

"You mean our house? Sure, G." After a pause, he asked, "Are you mad at me?"

"No, Sebastian. I'm shocked you never told me how you felt," I replied.

"When we get home, I want to make love to you and then go to bed. I'm really exhausted, G. Really … I am baby," he stated.

"Then maybe I'll respect your wishes and we can just go to bed," I replied.

"Seriously, Gina? We just went through this shit. Fuck, I'm tired, and I don't want to revisit it," he said, aggravated.

"I don't know what to say to you, Sebastian. Do you want me to say that I love you or that I respect you?" I asked.

"Say what is in your heart, G," he replied.

"I don't want to be the source of your disappointments."

"You're not. You need to understand where I'm coming from, that's all."

"Help me understand?"

"You want to understand me? Get to know me, G."

With his last comment, the conversation ended. I thought about what he'd said. I thought I knew him. How was I going to find out who he was? To me it was like living with a stranger at this point. He'd been different since he went sober. He was nicer, gentler, but now he seemed to be acting like I didn't really know him. I thought, Lex may be right in his assessment of Sebastian; he might be insane.

Sebastian pulled the car into the garage, and we went through the kitchen. I went to the fridge to grab some juice and poured a glass. I asked if he wanted some, to which he replied, "Just some in bed."

I noticed shades of old Sebastian appearing with that last comment; they kind of faded in and out of his new persona. He went upstairs, and I followed behind him. I got undressed and got under the covers. He put on the television and then threw the remote toward the end of the bed, pulling the covers back and rolling on top of me when he got in.

"I missed you," he said as he put his hand behind my ear and drew me in for a passionate kiss, driving himself into me with my assistance. I said nothing to him, because I needed to sleep on this new information I had just been handed at rehab. I made some noises of pleasure, and when he was ready to climax, I made a few more sounds. He got off and rolled over. Stroking his hair behind his head, he asked me what was wrong.

"Nothing. Can we start fresh in the morning?" I replied.

"Okay, babe. I don't want you pissed off at me," he stated,

"I'm not pissed off, Sebastian; I'm just confused. I want to be the girl you desire, not a disappointment," I replied.

"You don't get it, G. You really don't," he said.

"I love you, not your stage shit. I never cared about that," I said angrily.

"Let's go to sleep, G," he said.

"I love you. Goodnight," I replied.

"Night, G," he said.

"No I love you?" I asked.

"Fuck, G! Don't start. Go to sleep," he replied, aggravated.

I started crying, and he rolled over toward me, drying my tears and saying he was sorry. I had already forgotten that Michael had mentioned that Sebastian might have some anxiety after being released from rehab. It was to be expected. I put my arm around him and held him with compassion.

"Sebastian, I'm so proud of you for doing what you did. I respect your decision and commitment to stay off pills and drugs. I just want you to believe me," I said.

"I do believe you. Thank you for saying that to me, baby," he replied. As he pulled me toward him, his arm around me, he placed my head on his chest, stroking my hair. "I want you to understand my soul, G, 'cause that's where I'm fucked up, baby. Why do you think I gave it to you?" He paused as I looked up at him. "It was so you would protect it."

We said nothing more to each other. We just lay in complete silence with our bodies perfectly intertwined and fell asleep.

I woke up early the next morning. Sebastian was still sleeping. I put his robe on, because I liked the feeling of being wrapped in him, and headed downstairs to make coffee. Nigel came bouncing into the kitchen and asked if Sebastian was home. I invited Nigel to sit down for some freshly made coffee, offering to make him breakfast, but he said he had just eaten before coming over.

"No lass has ever cooked for him, only his mum. Were you privy to that?" Nigel asked me with a smile, not expecting an answer back. "You treat him right, Gina. He's a lucky bloke."

I thanked Nigel for his comment, because I knew that I did treat Sebastian well in many ways, with the exception of getting to know him, as I had been told the day before. I asked Nigel what Sebastian was really like.

"You mean at home?" Nigel asked, and I shook my head yes. "Ah, he's a quiet man. Keeps to himself. Before you, he had the wife. Never saw much of her. Whenever I did, I'd wish I hadn't. Didn't care much for that one, really."

Nigel told me about his disdain for the ex-wife and said that Sebastian seldom left the house when he wasn't on tour. He would occasionally go on holiday for a few weeks, but outside of that, Sebastian preferred to work in the comforts of his home studio, spending most of his time in there writing. I asked Nigel if he thought Sebastian felt compelled to always be working and making music and if that was the cause of him taking substances to deal with it.

"I suspect he started with that when the ex left him," Nigel stated.

"Why did she leave, Nigel? What was the reason?" I asked, curious.

"She took off when her modeling career did," Nigel replied.

"But there had to be another reason. What was it Nigel?" I asked, knowing there had to be more to the story that everyone was keeping a secret.

"He never told you, then?" Nigel asked with a raised eyebrow.

"No!" I replied, aggravated because I wanted to know the answer.

Nigel paused, looked at me, and moved in closer, whispering, "Your Sebastian came home early one afternoon and caught the slag in bed with another bloke. I came running over when I heard the windows shatter. I saw the bloke run out the kitchen door wearing nothing but his mind," Nigel said, laughing.

"Are you serious, Nigel?" I asked in shock.

"Can't make that up, love," Nigel said, as I took a sip of my coffee and pondered this insight into Sebastian's abandonment issues. I thought, *His ex really put him through it, and now I got to deal with the mess she left behind.*

It's All Greek to Me

It had been a few weeks since Sebastian come home from rehab, and everything was going well with him. Rick, Alana, and David came by the house for dinner. I had a hard time looking at Rick when they came through the kitchen door. I couldn't stop thinking about Rick and Emily doing each other. The visual on that was pretty unbelievable, only because Emily was a swaged-out party girl with a hard edge to her personality. She was abrasive and mean, not the type of person I could actually see Rick with. She was the polar opposite of Alana.

When Rick and Sebastian went out to the studio, I asked Alana if she had confronted Rick about his affair. With a puzzled look on her face she said, "Why would I do that? I just drop hints that I know. I mentioned that I saw Leon and that he was interviewing for a fashion thing with Emily in a few weeks. The look on Rick's face was, shall we say, expressive," Alana said, laughing.

I thought it was weird that Alana could somehow think that Rick's cheating was funny. Looking at her puzzled, I asked if things had settled down at home. She mentioned that Rick had not been out of the house "working" late for a few weeks.

The guys came in through the kitchen door as Alana and I were preparing plates for dinner. They sat down at the table, with David in a chair piled high with phone books so he could sit at the table with us. The guys thought it would be cute to take their forks and knives and start banging on the table like cavemen, saying they were hungry, and David mimicked them, trying to be just like one of the boys.

"Would you do that to your *mitera*?" I asked the cavemen, looking in their direction with a half-assed smile. They put down their cutlery and, with remorse, said they were just messing around. When the brothers got together, they were at times playful, but they could cross the line to being sexist pigs. This was one of those times.

Alana prepared David's plate and took it over to him, telling her son she didn't want him to pick up Daddy's bad habits. Rick smiled at her and changed the subject, looking toward Sebastian.

"Alana has been taking cooking classes. David and I are eating now. G does this for you all the time? *Mitera* will get jealous," he said with a smile toward me.

"I'm not in competition with your mom. I like to make Sebastian meals, and if he likes what I make and wants to eat, then that's great," I stated to the cheating, sexist pig, a.k.a. Rick, my brother-in-law.

"*Mitera* wants to show her how to cook Greek food. She showed Alana once. You both should let her come over, and she can teach you at the same time," Sebastian suggested. Alana did need to retake her Greek cooking class, and her relationship with Athene could be kicked up a notch or two. I found Sebastian's idea to be one of his better ones. He loved his mother's cooking, and he preferred her Greek food over the beef stew that I typically made for him.

We sat and babbled on for about ten minutes, and then the conversation took a rather unexpected turn when Rick blurted out in my direction, "So, I heard Leon got a gig with Emily. I didn't know they were tight."

"Leon has always wanted to work in fashion; he reached out to her," I replied.

"Did they hook up while he was here?" Rick asked with a raised eyebrow.

"No, but I know where you're driving this bus, Rick. Just put what you want to ask me on the table," I said.

"Whoa ... back up the bus, Gina," Rick replied, taken aback.

"I know where this is going, so let's cut the *s-h-i-t*," I said, spelling because David was sitting at the table. "I told you that I would never talk about you, and I haven't, so back your own bus up, Rick." I was really edged off because I had been put in the middle of his and Alana's issues.

"Gina, what are you talking about?" Rick asked.

"Emily is spilling your affair all over town, Rick," I said sternly.

"Affair? Are you joking right now, Gina?" Rick said in disbelief.

"Emily is the one who told Leon," I replied as Sebastian looked over at Rick, very confused.

"Emily said I was having an affair with her?" Rick asked, not backing down.

"She said you were making plans to be with her," I replied.

"What!" Rick shouted in shock, looking over at Alana.

"We're talking about Em, from the tour, right?" Sebastian asked, laughing.

"Sebastian, I told you that Leon was doing a gig with her. Don't act like you don't know who I'm talking about." I said, and Sebastian backed down. Then I turned to Alana. "You need to tell Rick everything. I want no part in these secrets." I looked sternly at her.

Sebastian was laughing and shaking his head at the thought of Rick and Emily together. Rick told everyone at the table that Emily was crazy to the tenth power and that he was not having an affair with her. I, having had enough of the lies, looked over at Alana and told her she needed to come clean with Rick about everything, put it all on the table.

Alana paused and looked at Rick with a serpent's smile. "*Les psemata*, Rick." (You lie, Rick.)

When she spoke Greek, Sebastian sat back in his chair shaking his head. Rick dropped his fork on his plate and leaned forward toward Alana, who was seated across from him, and Greek started flowing.

"*Ti xerete?*" (What do you know?) Rick asked Alana.

"*Arketa gia na sas chorisei.*" (Enough to divorce you.)

"*Poso kairo tha speek ellinika*, Alana?" (How long have you spoken Greek, Alana?)

"*Dedomenou pantremenos me sas.*" (Since I married you.) Alana gave Rick a blank stare.

Sebastian looked at me and said, "*Xerete elliniki*, Gina?" (Do you speak Greek, Gina?) But I didn't understand what he said. I just looked at him oddly.

"Well, Gina doesn't speak it," Sebastian replied, with a sigh of relief and a laugh.

"This is five cups of crazy you're hitting me with, Alana. I find out four years after we're married that you speak Greek. You learned that behind my back? That is some crazy-ass behavior," Rick said, highly aggravated at her. He was also clearly a tad bit freaked out by the Greek she spoke, because he never swore. "You're not taking my son from me, you hear me, Alana?" Rick stood up, banging his fist on the table at her.

David, hearing his parents yell, started crying, and Alana picked him up, telling him Daddy was mad at Mommy. Sebastian got up, grabbed Rick by the shoulder, and invited him outside as Rick continued looking at Alana and yelling at her. I pleaded with Alana to let me hold David while she and Rick were fighting.

Alana handed David over to me. By now, he was crying harder and he held on to me tight, bawling on my shoulder. I swiftly took David into the living room, and Sebastian again invited Rick outside to cool down. Alana followed me into the living room telling me that Rick was an asshole. Wanting to diffuse the situation, I asked Alana to go into the kitchen so I could calm David down. Alana wouldn't leave the living room; she stood there telling me she was happy that this part of her life was finally over and that she'd hated Rick's cheating and hated taking care of everything while he was gone on tour.

"It's going to be a long, hard fight to get David from me," Alana said.

"Alana, please. I'm trying to help David. This situation needs to calm down," I said.

Alana walked back into the kitchen to wait for Rick and Sebastian to come back into the house. I took David to the guest room, grabbed a toy I had brought back from New York for him, and started walking upstairs to my bedroom.

"David, let's go see what Aunt Gina got you in New York, okay?" I said. David was distracted, as he was holding on to his new toy.

I closed the bedroom door so David wouldn't hear the screaming that was now taking place in the kitchen. David and I were sitting on the bed, and he asked me why his mommy and daddy were yelling. I explained to him that sometimes mommies and daddies need to yell to feel better, just like how when he goes outside and yells, he feels better.

I turned on the television and put on a cartoon to drown out the fuck yous that were penetrating the bedroom wall. David and I lay on the bed waiting for the storm to pass. David was getting distracted by the fighting of his parents and wanted to know what they were yelling about downstairs. I turned to David and asked if he'd ever heard the story of Zeus. I was telling the story and didn't realize that Sebastian had come upstairs and was peeking in the door that he'd cracked open.

"I think we've had enough Greek for one evening," he said, smiling at the door. He walked in, and David stood up on the bed, wanting to be picked up by his uncle Sebastian. It melted my heart that he wanted his uncle to hold him. He was a little boy, and my heart went out to him. Sebastian asked me to help get David ready for bed, stating that he told Rick and Alana to let David stay the night to give them some space and time to sort out their mess.

I took David into the bathroom to wash up, and Sebastian went downstairs to find some of David's clothes in the hall closet. Finding a shirt and shorts, Sebastian came back upstairs and handed them to me, and I got David ready for bed. Sebastian picked him up and told him the monster would get him if he didn't get under the covers. David jumped into our bed and put the cover over his head. Sebastian cracked open the door, and asked me to hang out with David so he could go downstairs to check on the situation, which seemed to have cooled off.

Sebastian came back upstairs with a smile and said, "They left."

I was confused by this, because neither one of them had said goodbye to their son. Sebastian didn't seem bothered by the event, taking me by total surprise with his cavalier attitude about Alana and Rick's fight. Sebastian told me that they went through this after every tour; it was nothing new. They would go home, have a passionate time together, and then pick David up in the morning.

"What?" I said, looking at him confused.

"It turns them on, G. Whatever," Sebastian said as if he had seen this before.

"That's really messed up," I stated with a look of disgust.

"Really? No different than what we did to each other on the road, G. I didn't know she knew Greek, though; that's new," Sebastian replied, not really bothered by their behavior. He just shrugged it off.

"Did you know about Emily and him on tour?" I asked.

"Sorry he put you in the middle of it," Sebastian said nonchalantly.

"Emily told Leon she was in love with him and that he was getting a divorce," I said.

"Em is crazy if she thinks that, and Alana is a nutcase, G. This happens after every tour. You're going to have to do like the rest of us: play nice when they go through this crap, and don't get sucked into it," Sebastian said, blowing it off.

Someone was lying about the affair. It was either Rick or Emily, and I was more inclined to believe Emily's story over Rick's, given his track record. Rick got busted by Alana, and he confronted me about it, with Sebastian covering for his brother. It appeared to me that Rick had managed to sell Alana some lovey-dovey story about the news of his infidelity not being true, and this worked on Alana somehow. Alana knew about his extramarital affairs, but this was how she chose to cope with it—Rick sticking it to her really good on a child-free night. The only part about this story I did believe was that Rick and Alana would engage in a huge fight after every tour. Rick was well versed in the art of deception, and I had become wise to the touring game.

Sebastian went to the drawer and pulled out a pair of his shorts and one of his T-shirts, tossing them at me to put on. We always slept naked, but not this evening. We had a four-year-old to look after. Sebastian asked me to join him in the bathroom for a minute. Putting his arms around me, he said, "It's just for the one evening. Don't be too disappointed," smiling as he said it.

David fell asleep between us. When he did, Sebastian reached his arm over David to bring me into him for a kiss, telling me he couldn't wait to keep the monsters away for our own son.

The three of us were out cold when the phone started ringing at 5:00 a.m. I stumbled into a bedroom down the hall to answer it, thinking it may be David's parents, but no. It was Stan calling from the States wanting to speak to Bas. I told Stan that if he didn't want to get screamed at, he would wait three hours and then hung up the phone with Stan in midsentence before he could say anything else to me. Sebastian didn't wake up, which was a great thing. He would have been especially pissed off at Stan for calling at that hour.

At 9:00 a.m., Rick walked through the front door. The phone started ringing as he headed toward the kitchen. I was preparing David's breakfast and asked Rick to answer the phone, knowing good and well who it was.

"Hello?" Rick said, answering the phone. Then he looked over at me and rolled his eyes, confirming it was Stan.

Sebastian was still upstairs sleeping, so I sat down with David to feed him his breakfast. I could overhear Rick's phone conversation.

"Need to talk with the other guys about it. I'm not sure of anyone who would perform a rock opera, Stan. Gina is the only one I know who ever did that song … I'll have to talk to Bas and get back to you," he said before hanging up the phone.

"He called here at 5:00 a.m.," I said.

"Has he already talked to Bas?" Rick asked

"No, I told him to call back," I replied.

"That was a smart decision." Rick then changed the subject to the events that had unfolded the night before. "Hey, I want to apologize for last night. I'm aware that you know what's going on. Alana and I were not in a great space, but I'm not in love with Emily, Gina," he said because he got busted.

"Rick, I only care about Sebastian getting well and starting my own family with him. It's none of my business what you do, but I'll say, Alana has known for years about your activities on the road," I replied.

"Sorry you got dragged in it."

"Rick, I believe you will always find another Emily. I can't handle Sebastian finding another Laura. Your brother is the only one in this world who makes sense to me. If I lose him, I lose everything. I can't do DC again, Rick." I noticed Sebastian was standing, listing to our conversation, but Rick hadn't seen him.

"You know it doesn't mean anything, right?" Rick replied.

"And that's the problem. Where my guy puts his tool means everything to me, and I know Alana cares about yours too."

Sebastian walked into the kitchen, saying nothing to either one of us. He went over to pour a cup of coffee and then sat down next to David, teasing him that he was going to eat his eggs. I asked Sebastian if he wanted me to make him his own breakfast. With a grin, he said no and continued teasing David so he would eat.

Rick didn't let up on me. He thought it was easy for me and Sebastian, because I'd been on tour with them. Alana didn't tour. I countered that his reason for cheating didn't hold water, because Sebastian had cheated on me anyway. Sebastian interrupted, telling Rick to leave me out of his mess. Sebastian further insisted that Rick needed to figure out what he wanted to do with his life and his wife. Sebastian didn't want to be involved in his brother's marital problems anymore and was growing tired of their yearly theatrical meltdowns. Sebastian was more concerned about the negative effect it would have on David if Rick continued in his unhappy marriage.

"Figure it out. Seriously, Rick, stay or leave," Sebastian said.

"She'll get custody of David. I can't do it Bas," he replied.

"Then you've made a decision. Get her straight, Rick," Sebastian replied. Rick asked him to talk in private, and Sebastian said no, he was going to sit and drink his coffee. He invited his brother to sit and do the same.

"Stan called. Lex Lenord wants us to score his rock opera," Rick said, changing the subject.

"Let me guess … Lex is doing 'Lei Dorme' and wants Gina to be the lead," Sebastian said, laughing as he took a sip of his coffee.

'Yeah, pretty much," Rick said, subdued, as he leaned against the kitchen counter.

"I can see it as a rock opera if it's done right," Sebastian said as he teased David by tickling his stomach.

"You're serious? You want to score an opera?" Rick replied. He seemed shocked his brother would actually consider it.

"Where's your sense of adventure, Rick? I thought you liked that stuff. You begged Gina for weeks to do that stupid song," Sebastian replied with a smile.

"One song, not an entire opera. What about our next album?" Rick replied, disinterested.

"The music industry's changing. We need to think about how we're going to change with it." Sebastian paused and let out a sigh. "I need a break, Rick. The songs are already written; they just want us to Tin Garden the damn thing."

"We'll be sucked-up with Lex and this opera for months, Bas," Rick said. But seeing Sebastian was not backing down, he reluctantly gave up. "Fine, I'll call Stan and see what's on the back-end deal before we say yes to anything."

"We need to circle with Marcus and Chip about the plan with Stan, preferably before Gina and I head out on our honeymoon," Sebastian said.

"Where are you going?" Rick asked. I was looking over at Sebastian, wondering the same thing and waiting to hear where he was taking me.

"Santorini," Sebastian replied. Then he turned to me and smiled.

"When's that happening?" Rick asked, leaning against the counter with his arms and legs crossed.

"Tomorrow," Sebastian replied.

Rick hung his head, and I looked at Sebastian in shock. Sebastian, however, simply continued to play with David at the table, getting him to eat his breakfast. Rick went to the phone and made a call to Chip, who was in New York along with Marcus. I overheard Rick tell Chip that they needed to have a very impromptu band meeting. Then he made the call to Marcus, their drummer. Coming back into the kitchen, he told Sebastian that the call would take place in an hour. Sebastian went upstairs to take a shower and asked me to join him, leaving David and Rick downstairs.

We walked upstairs to our bedroom, and he shut the door.

Sebastian had wanted me to come with him because he figured Rick would start in again on me about his marriage issues but also because he wanted to take a sexy shower before dealing with his meeting. I asked Sebastian if we were really going on a honeymoon tomorrow, and he replied that his intention had been to tell me after Rick picked up David.

"I need some sun, G." he said, putting his arms around me and pulling me into him for a small little kiss. I told him that Leon was coming in later that same week. Sebastian said that Leon could stay there while we we're gone. "You'll see him when we get back." And we continued our sexy shower.

Sebastian and I got out of the shower and went downstairs. Rick was in the library with David watching television. They asked me to keep an eye on David as they headed out back to the studio to do their conference call. A few hours later, they both came into the kitchen laughing, just like old times. Rick commented that things should move in a more positive direction with the band now. Then he came into the living room and picked up David, whispering something in his ear and then putting him back down.

"Thank you, Aunt Gina, for my toy and for making me breakfast. I love you," David said, putting his arms around me. I felt his words melting my heart. David then ran to his Uncle Sebastian, and he picked him up. "I love you, Uncle Sebastian." They embraced in a tight hug. David didn't want to let go.

"I love you, buddy," Sebastian replied. Their bond was extremely tight. David was drawn to Sebastian's spirit and childlike qualities, as well as the love that Sebastian held for his family. It was the cutest thing I had ever seen.

Rick took David and left. Sebastian and I were alone. I looked at him with a smile and asked how things had gone in their meeting. Sebastian sat down on the couch and invited me to sit next to him. He said that Stan was still their manager for the day-to-day "T. G. ops," but he would be replaced by a tour management company for all future tours moving forward. He took my hand and, with a huge smile, told me that he would no longer have to deal with Stan. Rick had been designated as the voice of the band, putting him in charge of handling Stan directly. Sebastian would be able to focus on the creative and was officially removed from all future directly business-related discussions. That made him happy as a clam.

"How do you feel about Lex bringing 'Lei Dorme' to London?" Sebastian asked with an inquisitive smile.

"I knew he wanted to ask you guys to do it after I saw him in New York, but I had no idea he was bringing it to London," I said, surprised.

"I know; we spoke. I told Lex if he brought the production to London, I'd Tin Garden the fucking thing for him, but I'm not going to New York," Sebastian said as he put his arm over my shoulder.

"Are you serious? You guys are going to do it?" I asked, leaning into his chest.

"Sure, we could open ourselves up to a whole new audience, Gina," he replied.

"What about your current audience?" I asked,

"They ride or they don't, G. The audience doesn't decide what Tin Garden does creatively. I'm going with my gut on this one," Sebastian said. Then he mentioned that we needed to get packing for our trip back to Greece in the morning. He was looking forward to spending some time away in some warm weather.

Sebastian had his follow-up appointment with Michael at the rehab center in the afternoon. When he took off for London, I made a call to Leon and told him we were going on an impromptu honeymoon and that he was more than welcome to stay on at the house while we were gone. He could get the keys from Nigel. Leon teased me that he was going to enjoy being the queen of my castle while I was away, leaving us both laughing. I gave Leon the sordid details about the events that had unfolded with Rick and Alana the night before at my kitchen table, filling him in on the Greek dialogue Alana was spilling on it. Leon hadn't known that Alana knew Greek. Leon was on the other end of the phone howling.

"That man got caught in a Greek tragedy with his pants around his ankles. You be spilling some tea today, girl … No business!" Leon said, laughing hysterically.

"Rick could really do with some Jesus in his heart," I replied, snickering.

"Preach it, girl. Preach it. Take it to church … He's a mess with it," Leon said. He couldn't stop laughing. "You be giving me a story today… ooh."

After I got off the phone with Leon, I went to finish folding laundry. I heard Sebastian's sports car come up the driveway and pull into the garage just as I had pulled the last load of laundry from the dryer. Sebastian came in through the kitchen door and was in a great mood. He told me he wanted to ask a question of me. I stopped folding clothes and kept the thought in the back of my mind, *He just came back from rehab, so whatever he fires at me, I have to stay calm.* He put his arms around my waist, pulling me in closer to him.

"What would you say if I asked you to go off the pill now?" he asked with a smile. "I'm going to be off tour, and it's the perfect time. I want to be here for our son"

"What if we have a girl?" I asked, not wanting him to be disappointed.

"Don't worry, I'm only going to shoot you the Y chromosome," he said, laughing, as I hit him on the arm playfully.

"I'll officially go off the pill today," I replied with a smile.

"I want to be home to enjoy every minute. I'm doing the opera to put off another album for a while. It keeps me at home, G," he said. He continued on about how he wanted to enjoy our trip and really wanted us to connect with each other. He had my complete, undivided attention. I was captivated by this change in him. I thought, *Baby, I'm on board.*

The Honeymoon

Sebastian and I arrived in Athens, and was taken by surprise when the driver dropped us off at Pier 6, where we boarded a forty-one–meter yacht that had three levels and a full-time staff of twelve to cater to our every need. Sebastian had opted to charter a two-day trip on a private yacht to Santorini instead of taking a forty-five–minute flight.

The captain was on deck and introduced himself as we boarded. A senior crew member approached. The staff must already have been informed that Sebastian no longer drank, since they handed us juice and water. I looked at the juice in disappointment and asked if I could have an Amaretto Sour. The crew had to leave the boat and pick up a bottle before we left. I asked Sebastian if he minded me having a cocktail.

"You not pregnant yet, but I'm going to work on that this week," he said with a laugh. When one of the stewards came back with the Amaretto, we set out for the Aegean Sea.

The chief steward took Sebastian and I around the boat to show us where everything was, stopping at the grand room that had a piano. Sebastian sat down and began playing it for the crew, saying he would entertain them later. The senior steward walked us to our state-room, where our luggage was being unpacked by one of the crew members while our clothes were being carefully hung in the closet by another. The steward informed us that dinner would be served promptly at 8:00 p.m. Then the crew staff left the state-room, closing the door behind them to give us some private time alone.

Sebastian, with a look of lust in his eyes, moved toward me and started swiftly unbuttoning my shirt, yanking it off. He moved his hands over my bare chest, leaning in to kiss me on my neck. I had my hand strategically placed on the inside of his jeans, rubbing him as I started undoing the button.

"I want to fuck, Gina. Let's get crazy like we used to," he said. And we began to passionately make out.

I got the button undone on his jeans and slid my hands down the sides of his legs, taking his jeans with them. I knelt down on the floor, taking his number eight into my mouth. He placed his hands behind my head and was growing larger. I choked on him as I took him deeper down my throat. When he got hard enough, he pulled my head back and pulled me up from the subservient position, dragging me back toward the wall. Sebastian picked me up, took my skirt off, and placed my naked body on top of the dresser, spreading me open when he did. He had his hand on his rocket, and with little warning, he rammed himself into me, pounding his Johnson in me hard. Then he unexpectedly pulled out, grabbing me by the arm and throwing me down on the bed. He straddled me and inserted himself again, like a dog humping his favorite toy. He liked grabbing me under my knee and taking it up to the side of my face.

"Gina, come with me," he said in my ear as perspiration was dripping from every part of our bodies. Taking the back of my head, he pulled me in, kissing me as he came. After he got off and rolled over, he took my hand and held it to his chest. "I shot you a boy."

I was still catching my breath. I explained to him that getting pregnant would take a while. I 'd just gone off the pill. He turned over and put his face next to mine, kissing me.

"We can fuck again," he said with a laugh.

I was exhausted. We had not had hard sex like that in months, and I was sore from it.

"It felt different. I'd rather make love to you," he said, leaving me guessing whether his desire to "fuck" was vacation Sebastian or sober Sebastian wanting to see if he could still have hard sex without substances. Either way, this man definitely still knew how to fuck.

Our journey was well under way, and we put on our robes and opened up the balcony door to take in the sights of the sunset and enjoy the warm breeze, which was blowing the curtain back and forth on the door. The sounds of the ocean were peaceful and relaxing, just what we both needed. We were unreachable. We had no way of communicating with the outside world, and we loved it. We went out to the balcony and curled up on our chaise lounge, intertwined with one another. We lay there in silence until I started massaging his member through his robe. He turned his head toward mine, sliding his hand inside my robe, and we began making out, connecting without words. It was romantic, passionate, and peaceful. We could hear the sound of the waves crashing against the boat. He pulled me on top of him, leaning the chair back a bit when he did. He wanted me to climb aboard his mast, after which he turned me over on my back and boarded my vessel. And we made love on the balcony in the chaise lounge. We were connected and in love and didn't want the moment to end. We talked about sleeping out there that night but ended up taking a shower and getting ready for dinner.

It was nearly eight o'clock when we finally emerged from our state-room, heading up the stairs to deck 3 for dinner. We were met by the chief steward, who informed us that a traditional Greek meal of *giouvetsi* would be served. I was not a fan of lamb. The steward must have known that, since he then added, "And for Madam, we have the grilled swordfish." I was relieved, I didn't want to have to ask them to make me a grilled cheese sandwich; that would have been embarrassing for Sebastian.

We were served a six-course meal that took two hours to finish. We sat, in love, at a table that was lit by candlelight. Sebastian took my hand and looked into my eyes. "God, how happy are you right now? Do you have any idea how much I love you?" he asked as he propped his elbow on the table, putting his hand to the side of his face and smiling at me.

"I've never been happier. I know it wasn't always easy, but there's not another person in this world who would have been assigned to me. You're my person, Sebastian. I love you," I said, putting my hand to his face as he leaned in for a kiss.

Dinner finished, and we went into the grand room. The crew wanted to hear Sebastian play a few songs on the piano before going to bed. He was only too eager to oblige. When he was engaged with people wanting to hear him play, it brought him out of his shell, since he typically lived most of his life inside his own head. Since going through his treatment program, he'd begun opening up more and interacting with people, and I loved this side of him. He was happy.

Sebastian sat down at the piano, playing around, and asked if anyone had any requests. He pretended like he didn't know how to play the piano, hitting the keys and making noise. The crew wanted to hear "Wait till I'm Home," of course, and after he finished it, they were all excited and wanted more. Sebastian started playing pieces of songs everyone knew, marrying them together. When he stopped, one of the stewards asked him to play "Loves Lies Bleeding." Sebastian paused and with a funny stare.

"You know that's Elton's, right?" Sebastian snickered. Then he asked the steward to open all the windows so he could get the breezy wind effect to set the mood before adding, "I'm just kidding. I don't know it." Everyone sighed in disappointment.

Then Sebastian got a serious look on his face, showing me four fingers and pointing in my direction. He started playing the first notes of Funeral for a Friend. The room let out a gasp and then got silent. The captain must have heard the music, because he came down during the intro and asked if Elton had jumped on board. Sebastian continued the song, singing the words, with everyone joining in on the chorus. It was met with thunderous applause. Of course. It's Elton's.

After Sebastian finished on that high note, he told the crew that he had a new song, asking if they wanted to be the first to hear it. One of the stewards said, "Are you kidding? Yes, we want to hear it." I looked over at Sebastian puzzled. I didn't know he had a new song, but I had been off the Tin Garden reservation for a while.

He sang, "An exit to be on your own, circumstances never faced alone. Decisions you made, intention to be gone before you could think. Standing there wanting more, there was an open door. Make you stay? Isn't it time you were on your way? In a heart, there is no doubt. Illusion's what it's about. You see the road when you leave …"

Sebastian finished his interesting song and the crew applauded. I thought, *Interesting lyrics*. I presumed it had been written about me when we were going through our crap. The steward asked him the name of it.

"It's called 'Leave,'" Sebastian replied. *Ding, ding.* I was correct. He got up from the piano and said that he could take requests tomorrow, but for this evening, we were headed to our room. The chief steward asked Mr. Roland if we would like breakfast brought to our room in the morning, and both of us nodded yes. But we told him to bring it late; we wanted to sleep in. We suggested the crew do the same. The crew thanked him for the songs, and Sebastian told the captain, "Seriously, let them sleep in tomorrow." That comment was met with a standing ovation, and we headed downstairs to our state-room.

When we got to our room, I opened the balcony door, and we lay down on the bed still in our clothes. We were captivated by the sound of the sea hitting the boat. I put my head on Sebastian's chest, and he held me close. The fresh air knocked him out; he fell asleep in a matter of minutes. I laid on his chest, feeling his heart beat and recalling the lyrics to his new song and the letter he'd written in rehab. I had finally figured out his "I don't know him" issue, but he was sound asleep.

Sebastian and I were awoken by a knock on the door. The stewards brought our breakfast to the room. We were still in our clothes from the night before. Sebastian was surprised he'd passed out without being high. Removing his clothes, he put on his robe, and we took our breakfast outside on the balcony. It was a beautiful, sunny day, warm, with a slight breeze blowing off the deck. We could hear the sounds of boats passing on the water. I had been brought fruit and yogurt, and he'd gotten a heartier meal of Greek staka and eggs. Yuck.

As I was taking a bite of melon, I looked over at him. "Sebastian, I understand now," I said.

Sebastian had just taken a bite of his breakfast. "What is it that you understand. Gina?" he replied, taken off guard.

"You, Sebastian. I understand what you said to me in rehab. You express yourself in the written word. You have a disdain for one-on-one communication," I replied.

"Took you that long?" he said, with a sideways glance.

"Sebastian, where did the pain come from?" I asked, curious.

"Being fucked over," he replied. He clearly wanted to drop the subject.

"By me or your ex?" I asked, hoping for the correct answer.

"The ex," he replied. There was a hint of aggravation in his voice.

"She was the love of your life, wasn't she?" I asked, anticipating his reply.

"She was, until I met you. Does that bother you?" he asked. The expression on his face seemed to say, "How dare you ask me this question?"

"No, because it's honest," I replied, not really happy with his reply.

"I don't love her. I love you. The only thing you could do to fuck this up would be to fall in love with someone else," he said with a serious look.

"Loving someone else wouldn't even enter my mind, Sebastian," I replied. I was shocked he could even ask a question like that.

"I know, I'm your Greek god. You worship me. That made me wonder if you were really in love with me or the rock star," he replied sarcastically.

"I love you, Sebastian, what's inside. I never loved that stage crap or the cock-rocker bullshit. I hate every part of it," I said defensively.

"But that's who you fell in love with, Gina," he stated matter-of-factly.

"Sebastian, I fell in love with you and probably your pain. I wanted to save you from it," I replied lovingly.

"I had to save myself, G." He paused. "Now that you understand me, do you still want me?" he asked with a snicker.

"I'm not revisiting the tell-me-you-want-me talk," I said aggravated.

"Are you in love me, or are you in love with the Greek god?" he asked playfully.

"I'm in love with Sebastian Adonis Roland, who lives in Surrey," I replied in a serious tone.

"Do you know how happy I am that you finally understand this? Christ, it took long enough, but I get it. You're a tactile processor; it takes you longer." He went back to eating, trying to drop this subject.

"Why do you say I'm a tactile processor?" I asked, not knowing what that was.

"Because you associate everyday objects with people. Your mind drifts," he said in a slightly raised tone of voice.

"Is that a bad thing?" I asked somberly.

"No, it just takes you a hell of a lot longer to process information. I didn't say you were dumb; it's just that you have to feel it and touch it before you understand it. I get it."

I glanced over at him, wanting to continue our little interesting and insightful discussion, but he would have preferred writing a song about it. Maybe his next hit would be called "Tactile Processor" on the new album from Tin Garden called *Your Mind Drifts*. I had to face it; he preferred to communicate in the written and physical format. My Mr. Mysterious did not seem so complicated to me any longer. I continued looking at him as he ate, processing how I would get him to write me a tactile note every day so we could communicate on a daily basis.

Tin Garden Does *Lei Dorme*

It had been four months since we came home from the honeymoon. Sebastian and I had had a great time in Greece, where we spent most of the day laying out in Santorini on our balcony and having sex. We both came home happy and tan, and our communication was getting better. I even got him to write me little notes every day by telling him I was making a scrapbook for our future children. He was only too eager to indulge me in it. He would always leave the notes on the kitchen counter, where I would see them when I first woke up, writing them before he came to bed. One of them read, "The day I met you was the day my life changed forever. I love you. Sebastian." And there was the occasional funny one, like "I sat here wondering how you got so damn lucky. Guess who loves U?" after which he had drawn a happy face.

But one particular morning, I went to the kitchen, all happy to get my daily love note and wondering if it would be funny or romantic, but I found this instead: "G, we have $, spend a few more £s and get better coffee. Italian? Oh yeah, love you. S. xoxoxo." I did keep that one; I kept them all.

Leon had stayed on with us for a few weeks after we got back from Greece. He'd gotten a full-time gig in London with Emily and was currently back in New York sorting out things so he could move over here before his next fashion event. Leon had just received his work sponsorship visa before he left and was getting established in the world of fashion, making connections through Emily.

Leon was working on his own clothing line on the side called L. T., taking the initials of his name, Leon Taylor. It was a women's couture line inspired by the streets of New York. Leon also wanted to do a more affordable line called L. T. N. Y. for those girls who could not spend a thousand dollars on a dress. Sebastian and I were really happy for him and his decision to make the move over to focus on his own line.

Bridgette had put in a bid for the London-to-Milan route and was waiting for that to go through. Either way, she would be leaving New York and moving back to Italy, pleasing her parents. Her prospects were looking good; she would likely be based out of Milan and would get a crash pad in London. Leon and I were ecstatic that she was going to be closer.

Sebastian had started work on the rock opera *Lei Dorme* and was spending most of his time in the studio with Lex. Carl had just gotten into town and was getting everything ready for the auditions that were taking place in London, as the production was getting closer to being finished. Lex and Sebastian were always in the studio working, putting the finishing touches on the music, and translating the opera from Italian into English. I hardly ever saw Lex or hung out with him during this time. Sebastian's studio was just like an office, only his was full of instruments and a mixing board. I never popped in to the studio unannounced. I only went over there if he called up to the house and asked me to come over or if he and Lex needed me to sing to work out some of the arrangements they had been working on.

One afternoon, Carl came by the house to pick up Lex, and he and I started chatting and getting caught up with things back home in New York as he waited for Lex to emerge from the studio, or The Cave, as it was called. Carl was regaling me with a crazy story about how Lex was going to ask me to do the lead role in the opera. I told Carl that it would be impossible. Sebastian would never go for it, because we were trying to have a baby. Sebastian had taken the gig with Lex so he could work at home in case I did get pregnant. I couldn't exactly go back to the theater working Lex's schedule of twelve- and fifteen-hour days. Just as I was telling Carl no way, Sebastian and Lex came in through the kitchen door.

"Oh, there you are. Having afternoon tea and crumpets?" Lex said, making Carl snicker. "We have a meeting with wardrobe in an hour; it'll take that long to get down this driveway." Lex laughed.

"It'll take me that long to put you in your chair and roll you to the car," Carl said to Lex with an attitude, and I started laughing.

"Aren't we a pissy little queen today?" Lex said with his hands folded toward Carl.

"I work for you. It's been a hard life," Carl replied, unamused by Lex's comment.

"The only thing hard for you has been your outlook on life. That's why you can't find a hard thing to put in it," Lex said with an upward inflection in his voice.

"Why are you so hateful to me?" Carl said, looking at Lex with a frown.

"Hateful? I'm trying to help you, dear. Lose the pissy attitude," Lex said, unapologetic.

Sebastian was standing there watching the ping-pong match between the two of them and trying not to laugh. It was typical Lex and Carl banter; they always brought joy to so many wherever they went. I did miss the back-and-forth between them. It was like being in the theater again, but without the twelve-hour rehearsals.

Lex said he had a question he wanted to ask me. I knew what it was and said, "Lex, the answer is no. I can't Sebastian and I are trying to have a baby."

"Gina, this is your swan song. I mean, literally, it is," Lex said with a chuckle.

Sebastian glanced in my direction with a look of relief when I declined. He told Lex that my decision had been made and to move on and find someone else.

After Carl and Lex left, Sebastian's mother called. She was on her way over to give me a Greek cooking class, my tenth since the honeymoon. Alana had opted out of learning to cook with us; she and Rick were still going through their issues. Alana had put divorce back on the table a few weeks prior, and when she did, Sebastian told me we were staying out of it.

Athene came in through the kitchen, bringing all of the items needed for Moussaka, a dish of minced meat, tomatoes, onions, cheese, and béchamel sauce. It was a dish she prepared often, and it was her baby's—I mean, Sebastian's—favorite. Athene was pleased that I was taking an interest in learning how to make her dishes.

Sebastian told his mother he was happy that I was making the effort to learn. We'd begun cutting up all the things to layer into the baking dish when I started feeling dizzy, telling Athene I needed to sit down. Athene put the dish into the heat storage stove.

"Gina, what's wrong?" Athene asked, walking over where I was sitting on the kitchen chair.

"I don't know. I'm really dizzy," I said as I folded my arms and put my head down on the table.

"Gina, did you eat today?" Athene asked.

I couldn't remember if I had or not. "Yeah, but I don't know. Something's not right," I said, incoherent.

"Where's Sebastian?" Athene asked in a raised voice.

"In the studio," I replied, feeling flush and sick.

Athene ran outside, yelling for Sebastian. I passed out. When I came to, Sebastian was holding me in his arms, yelling at his mom to call 999 (the emergency number in England). His mother told Sebastian she was on hold with them.

"Gina, baby, wake up. What's wrong, baby? *Mitera* I'm taking her to Royal. Grab my keys on the counter," Sebastian said in a panic, picking me up and yelling to his mom to pull the car out of the garage. His mom ran outside and backed the car from the garage, yelling at him to be careful. They didn't know if I had hit my head or what had happened to me. He put me in the car, asking his mother to stay at the house, and made the short drive to hospital.

Upon arriving, Sebastian pulled up to the emergency door, left the car running, and flagged down an intake person to admit me. It was very chaotic and confusing. I passed out again. Sebastian had his hand to his head, sitting in a chair next to me, when I started waking up, wondering where I was.

"Where am I?" I asked. My vision was blurry.

Sebastian jumped up from the chair and bent over, putting his arm around me. "Baby, what happened?" he asked with a lowered voice.

"I don't know, Sebastian. I was cooking …" I began, but at that moment the doctor walked in. He told Sebastian that they had run all the necessary tests and then asked if we were married. Sebastian, with a funny look, said yes and then asked why.

"Wanted to make sure. There's nothing seriously wrong with her. Anemia," the doctor said with a small smile on his face.

Sebastian cut him off, angered. "What do you mean? She passed out. There is something wrong with her."

"The only thing wrong with her is that she is depleted of iron and needs some rest … but also, she's pregnant," the doctor said, with a smile in my direction.

"What? Seriously?" Sebastian said as a smile spread across his face.

"I'll get the paperwork for her discharge. She's to have several days of bed rest, no walking. Anemia was the cause of the fainting. It's common in pregnancy. She needs to eat meat to sort out her iron," the doctor said before leaving the room for the discharge paperwork.

"Baby, you're pregnant! G, we're going to have a baby!" Sebastian said excitedly. He then put his arms around me. I was in disbelief.

The shock had just set in. Yeah, we'd been having a lot of sex, and yes, I was off the pill, but I was still having my period. I'd had no reason to think I was pregnant. When I told Sebastian it was impossible that I was pregnant because I was still having my period, he said that he would tell the doctor that when he came back. While we were waiting for my discharge papers, Sebastian made a call to the house. As he dialed the number, he said that he was going to wait until the family got together before he told anyone the news, but he wanted his mother to have dinner ready when we got home.

"*Mitera*, Gina's okay … That thing you made, does it have meat in it? She needs to eat meat; her iron is low. See you in an hour. Stay there; don't leave," he said before hanging up the phone.

Sebastian's enthusiasm waned when the doctor came back in to release me. He took over the conversation. "You said she is pregnant, but she's still having her period," Sebastian said, worried.

The doctor said he was putting me on bed rest for a week and to follow up with my doctor soon, but I was being discharged from his care. Sebastian seemed somewhat relieved, and we were both too happy to be getting out of there.

I was put into a wheelchair and taken to the front door, where Sebastian had the car pulled up. He got out of the driver's seat and gently held my hands, helping me in. He was treating me like a fragile flower.

"I'm fine, Sebastian," I said as he got back in the driver's seat.

He pulled forward and turned off the car. Then he leaned over and pulled me toward to him. "We're going to be parents, G," he said as he put his head to mine with tears in his eyes. We sat in the car, both in shock. "I'm going to be a dad." He took his shirt sleeve and wiped the tears from his eyes.

When we got home, he opened the car door, picked me up, and took me into the kitchen. I asked him to put me down, and he reminded me that the doctor said I had to stay off my feet. His mother and father were in the library room watching the BBC.

"*Mitera*," Sebastian yelled, and they both came running into the kitchen.

"Why are you holding her, Sebastian?" Richard asked, concerned.

"I have to take her to bed. *Mitera*, come and help. Dad, wait here. I have to get her ready for bed," Sebastian said. Athene followed behind Sebastian, telling him to be careful not to fall down the stairs. I again asked Sebastian to put me down, and he said no way. He asked his mother to pull the covers back from the bed and to get a robe. Athene was frantically looking for a robe as Sebastian gently helped me out of my clothes.

"*Giagia* (grandma), do you have that robe?" Sebastian asked. His mother came running out of the bathroom with a look of shock holding the robe.

"Richard!" Athene yelled down the hall, and Sebastian threw me the robe to put on. Richard ran up the stairs.

"What in God's name is going on, Sebastian?" Richard said angrily.

"*To moro mou echei ena moro!*" (My baby is having a baby!) Athene started yelling. She was in tears and threw her arms around Sebastian.

"Would someone tell me in English what in God's great name is going on in this house?" Richard said sternly to Sebastian and Athene, looking at them both.

"Okay, Grandpa, calm down," Sebastian said with a laugh, looking at his dad.

"Sweet Jesus. Say it's so. Congratulations son," Richard said with a smile plastered on his face. He went over and hugged his boy.

I could not believe what I was hearing. I sat back in the bed, watching this drama unfold between the three of them. They spoke of blessings, miracles, and me being chosen by God to carry the baby of their golden boy, Sebastian. I thought, *What in the hell—I mean, heaven—am I watching? The International Baby Breaking News on the second coming of Jesus?* You would have thought so by the way they were carrying on. Sebastian asked his mother to bring me some meat and also requested that she come over every day and help with meals. I thought, *Fantastic. This is going to be a long pregnancy.*

Athene went downstairs to make a plate of food for me—the meal we had started to prepare before I passed out. Athene told Sebastian that he needed to watch over me on this "special evening" and that she would be back in the morning to make meals that could be warmed up and brought to me in bed. I was grateful to have his mother's help, but his parents were being highly indulgent of Sebastian's behavior and the baby news.

After Athene and Richard left, I was exhausted, not from the shock of being pregnant but from the commotion that had taken place. I'd wanted to make sure everything was okay with the baby first before the Greek blasted off his big mouth to his parents. I'd had no plans of telling anyone I was with child until after I saw my doctor.

Sebastian told me he would be taking me to the doctor's office in the morning. As he got into bed, I called out to my Greek god, and he replied that that wouldn't work on him this evening. He got out of bed and walked to his dresser.

"We're not having sex until you see the doctor," he stated firmly, leaving me disappointed. He returned wearing of a pair of boxers and his dirty-dog T-shirt, which he decided to throw on to curtail my enthusiasm for his wiener. He leaned over and kissed me goodnight, placing a gentle hand on my stomach and saying how much he loved me and our baby. I knew at that moment that Our Very Erotic and Romantic sex days were O. V. E. R.

At eight o'clock, I woke up to the sound of closing doors and Sebastian walking around the house with heavy feet. I was still exhausted from the hospital drama and was barely awake when he said we needed to go. Sebastian had called the doctor to make an appointment for me to see him right away. I got out of bed, and Sebastian barely let me brush my teeth.

We got into his car and headed toward London. He told me in the car that he wanted everything to be okay and that he was worried. But I was surprised when he started in on my eating habits.

"If anything happens to our baby … Do you see why it's so important to eat? I'm going to force food into you, I swear, G," he said, angry that I didn't eat properly.

I was tired from the night before and in no mood for Sebastian's mouth, so I turned on the radio.

"Damn it, G, this is my baby too. How in the fuck can you not care?" he said, turning off the radio.

"I do care, Sebastian," I replied, submitting to him. I did not want to argue.

"I'm not playing with this food issue anymore. You will start eating," he said, pulling the car over. "Gina, if you have an eating disorder, please fucking tell me." He looked directly into my eyes.

"I don't have an eating disorder, Sebastian. I just don't like meat," I replied.

"This is our baby. Learn to like it. Goddammit, you can really piss me off," he said, aggravated, as he pulled the car out fast back onto the road.

"I don't want to piss you off. I'll do whatever the doctor tells me to do. It's not like I knew I was pregnant, Sebastian," I replied, upset.

"What you're carrying is precious cargo. I'm on edge. Sorry," he said, taking my hand and holding it in his lap.

We made a speedy trip into London. Sebastian instructed the

doctor's office to have a wheel chair ready for me when he pulled up. I was greeted at the door and swiftly taken in to see the doctor. Sebastian, after parking the car, quickly came into the room where I was waiting, slamming the door behind him. Causing a scene at 8:30 a.m. was only drawing attention to himself.

"Sebastian, please stop. You are making me nervous," I said, highly anxious at his behavior.

"I'm sorry, baby. I'm worried," he replied, nervously pacing the floor.

"If your behavior is any indication of what you will be like when I deliver this baby, it will stress me out Sebastian," I said, asking him to sit down and relax.

"Sorry, G." He pulled up a chair and sat, bouncing his left leg up and down.

"Calm down," I said as the doctor walked into the room. Sebastian took over the conversation. He was very on edge about me still having my period. I was worried, but I didn't want Sebastian to see that. It would only stress him out even more, and that was a trigger for him.

Sebastian was asked to stay behind when I was taken off to an exam room. I informed the doctor that it was important to have my husband with me, explaining his triggers to substance abuse. The doctor looked at me with understanding and had the nurse go and get Sebastian.

I was having blood drawn from my arm when Sebastian entered the room. He was asked to wait in the chair, and he sat fidgeting in it. Sebastian kept asking questions of the doctor about the tests they were going to do. The doctor answered his questions with the patience of a saint.

After about an hour of tests, the doctor came back and told us that I was indeed anemic but that the ultrasound would show them more. The doctor hooked up the machine, and for the first time, Sebastian and I were able to see a faint image of our baby. The doctor was able to determine that I was about ten weeks pregnant. He placed his stethoscope to my tummy and said, "I hear the heartbeat." He invited Sebastian to take a listen. Sebastian put the ear piece in and moved the round metal piece over my stomach, pausing when heard the heartbeat and smiling.

The doctor informed me that bed rest was mandatory for a few days. He told me to bring my iron levels up and come back immediately if the bleeding continued. I was more interested in whether I could have sex with my husband. The doctor replied, "If you feel like it and want to, then by all means."

I glanced at Sebastian with a look that said, "I'm getting some of you tonight." He just shook his head and leaned back in his chair with the look of being unimpressed. I also asked how long we should wait to tell anyone about our news. He told us that three months was the appropriate time to make an announcement. Our baby was due in December, based on the date of my last period, which I had to guess at.

When we left the doctor's office, Sebastian was over-the-moon happy and relieved. In the car, Sebastian suggested that we stay downstairs in the guest room while I was on bed rest, so we didn't have to go up and down stairs.

When we pulled into the driveway, he told me he would get my things and bring them to the guest bedroom. When he came back with his robe, I asked him to come lay down with me before he went to his studio. He did, but he told me that having him would need to wait until later. He leaned over and gave me a hug. I felt that Sebastian was treating me differently.

"We have been through it the last twenty-four hours," he said, holding my hand.

"I don't want to turn you off," I said, crying tears of exhaustion and relief.

"Turn me off? I love you, Gina. You're carrying my baby. If that's not love, I don't know what is," Sebastian said, letting me cry on his chest.

I began crying even harder. "I'm going to get big. You'll never want to have sex again."

"Gina, I can't wait to see you get bigger. Are you kidding?" he said with a smile.

"Then why don't you want to make love to me?" I asked, crying.

"It's not that I don't want to. I don't want to hurt you or our baby. Gina, please don't cry," he said, holding me.

"I love you, Sebastian, and I don't want you to find someone like Rick did," I replied.

"Baby, you and I are forever. You know my brother knocked Alana up before they got married, right?" Sebastian said.

I gave him a look of shock. "No," I replied, confused.

"We built our foundation, Gina; they didn't. Alana and my mom don't really see eye to eye because of that," Sebastian said, trying to make me feel better.

"I kind of got the impression they didn't get along," I replied.

"My parents love you. They love Alana too but because of David. It's different. They see you as the one who saved my soul, Gina," he said, looking into my eyes.

"You told me that you had to save yourself," I said, recalling his comment on our honeymoon.

"I went to rehab because of what you said to me about starting a family. You were right," he said with a smile. Then he gave me a kiss.

Sebastian convinced me to take it easy for the rest of the day. He put on the television, insisting that I should close my eyes and get some rest. He left and went to his studio, coming back after an hour to check on me. He was cute as he peeked into the room, smiling before closing the door.

I heard a car pull up outside and someone coming through the kitchen, heading up the stairs to the bedroom, and calling out my name when I wasn't there. It was Athene. I called for her to come to the guest bedroom. Athene came in with a tray of food. I was so grateful for her help with meals. I mentioned to Athene that she could probably catch Sebastian out in the studio. Athene said that she'd tried but that he wasn't there. I thought that was odd and asked if the car was in the garage, but she said it was gone.

Athene decided to stay at the house until Sebastian came home, wanting to know why her son would leave his wife at the house by herself after all the doctor drama. I suggested that maybe he had gone to the store, but Athene interjected and said that her son should have asked Melba to come over until he returned.

Athene took a seat in the guest bedroom chair and waited for a few hours. At five thirty, Sebastian came walking through the back door. Athene, tearing out of her chair, stormed into the kitchen. Greek was echoing through the halls as Sebastian walked into the guest bedroom with his aggravated *mitera* behind him. Sebastian handed me a present, ignoring his mother, and I sat up to open it. Athene looked at Sebastian as if in a standoff and told him in English not to leave the house unannounced.

"*Mitera*, I got it. I won't do it again," Sebastian replied as I started opening the box. Inside sat a tiny dirty-dog T-shirt just like his.

Looking at it, I said, "And if it's a girl?"

He smiled, shaking his head no. Athene saw Sebastian's mini-me shirt and tore into him.

"Sebastian Adonis, you left Gina in the house for that?" she said, shaking her head at him in disappointment.

Sebastian was happy about his gift for the baby, telling his mother that she needed to be happy too because he was sure we were having a boy. His mother wasn't indulging his behavior this time. She took a very firm stance and stated that he needed to look after his wife. The T-shirt could have waited. With a peculiar look on her face, she asked the name of the store where it had been purchased. Sebastian, looking at his mother, brazenly replied that it hadn't been purchased at a store; it had come from his wardrobe contact.

Hearing that, I knew he'd gone to see Emily. I was confused about why he would reach out to her, knowing that Rick was having some sort of affair with her. Sebastian said that he'd wanted to get to the bottom of the story she was telling and had used the T-shirt as an excuse to talk with her. Athene, listening to his explanation of the T-shirt, was aggravated and started in on him again.

"I don't like these group-girls that chase my boys," Athene said.

"Groupies, *Mitera*," Sebastian said, correcting his mother.

I couldn't believe he was dropping this T-shirt bomb on me and his mother. He hadn't taken into consideration how it might affect my thinking patterns or how Emily may have tried to give him a freebie and service him while I was down for the count—easy pickings, as it were. I was aggravated that he'd snuck out of the house, but I sat in silence so Sebastian could explain his goat-rope story.

"I wanted the shirt; she designed it. But I also wanted to know what she's been saying about Rick. He is my brother," Sebastian replied pointedly.

Athene and I sat listening to his explanation. It was a T-shirt with the sexist double entendre, which I made known to him. He snapped back that it was rock 'n' roll and where was my sense of humor? Athene started in on him again, only this time in Greek, so I had no idea what was being said. As Sebastian and his mother were going at it, the phone rang. I answered as the Greek banter got louder in the background. Finally, they took it to the hallway. It was Rick.

"G, I hear my mother. Is Bas there?" Rick asked, very subdued.

"Yes. What's wrong Rick?" I asked.

"I need to talk to Sebastian. Alana and David were in a car accident," Rick said, fighting back tears as he was telling me.

"Oh my God!" I yelled. Sebastian came running into the room. "Alana and David were in a car accident," I said, nervously handing him the phone. Sebastian paused, looking at me visibly confused, and ripped the phone from my hand.

He started speaking with Rick, shaking his head. "I'll be there in five," Sebastian said. He paused and looked over at his mother. "We have to go. It's serious." His mother, who was horrified, began asking Sebastian a million questions. I started to get out of bed, but Sebastian insisted that I needed to stay home.

"I'm going, Sebastian. I'll call your dad and meet you there," I said, heading toward the hall bathroom.

Sebastian and his mom were in the hall, grabbing keys and speaking loudly on their way out the front door as I made the call to his father. I told him about the accident and told him to get over to Royal Hospital. Richard was upset, wanting to know more, but I explained that Athene and Sebastian had just left the house and that I was following behind them.

I took a fast, working-class shower, brushed my teeth, and headed out the door. When I got to the emergency room, I found Sebastian, Rick, and Athene speaking with a doctor. As I approached, Rick bent over and started crying. I walked over, and Athene hovered over Rick, who was bent over. Sebastian sat down in a chair next to Rick and put his hand on his brother's.

"What is going on?" I asked. Sebastian stood up and walked me over to the side of the room.

"David's in critical condition. Alana's gone, Gina," Sebastian said, standing frozen and in shock. I was immediately transported to a paralyzed state of disbelief. Then I turned to look over at Athene, who was holding on to Rick. I saw the doctor come back and broke from Sebastian, stopping the doctor in the hallway.

"Has he seen his child yet? He needs to see his child," I demanded of the doctor.

The doctor said that he would send someone to get Rick to take him to see David once they had him stabilized. My range of emotions went from sadness to anger in a matter of a few seconds. Looking down the hall, I noticed the chapel and said I needed to say a prayer, suggesting that Sebastian follow me and do the same. I insisted that saying a prayer for David was the only thing to help in this situation. I then left Sebastian's side and walked down the hall toward the chapel. Approaching the cross, I got to my knees and called on Archangel Michael for protection of David, taking my hands and folding them into the prayer position as tears streamed down my face. I asked God to spare David's life, because he was just a little boy.

I was bent down in front of the altar, praying with my eyes closed, when I felt someone kneel beside me. I looked over with tears streaming down my face. It was Sebastian. I leaned my head toward his shoulder, acknowledging him, and went back to prayer.

Sebastian and I were both praying when Athene walked in and approached us from behind. I stood up. Sebastian had his hands still locked in prayer, looking down at the railing. He told his mother not to say anything bad. Athene was anxious and said that Rick was with David. She said to come to the waiting room when we were done. We stood up and left the chapel. In the waiting area, Richard had just arrived and was sitting with Athene. Sebastian and I took the open seats next to each other across from his parents.

"If anything happens to him, Gina ..." Sebastian said, angered.

"Sebastian, David needs you to stay positive. Please do that for him," I said, taking his hand. Sebastian let go of my hand, bent over, and put his hands to his forehead. I put my arm around his back stroking him for comfort.

The doctor came back into the waiting area. Richard jumped from his seat when he saw him walk toward us. Sebastian was detached when the doctor said, "We won't know the extent of injuries until the child wakes up. He's stabilized. He's a lucky boy; his mother had him in a car seat. A grief counselor will come to sort out questions. Take all the time you need."

The doctor left. Nobody could say anything. We had more questions than answers. It was confusing how it had even happened. Sebastian turned toward me and asked me to take his mother and go back to the house to start all the necessary calls, the first being to Stan. He wanted to minimize any public awareness of the news. He also wanted his mother to contact Alana's only living family member, an uncle named Martin. It was going to be a long night. Athene was distraught and only wanted to see David. The hospital would only allow Rick to be with his son, and he was staying with the boy until he woke up. The trauma of waking up in a hospital with no familiar faces was bad enough. I couldn't imagine receiving the news about losing his mother at the age of four without Rick being there for him.

Athene told Sebastian that she would stay the night at our house and asked him to call when David woke up. She wanted to be there to see her grandson. Sebastian agreed but reiterated that he wanted her and me to start making all of the calls, because it would take time.

Athene and I arrived back at the house. Once we entered, I led her to the office where Sebastian had all his personal contact numbers. Athene made the call to Alana's uncle. I went upstairs to give her some privacy for that difficult call and made the business calls to Stan and Lex to tell them what had happened. I decided not to call Andy or Joe from Raiders, because if I did, all of England would know in a matter of a few minutes. We had to minimize the information going out.

I placed a call to Leon, knowing it was early in the States. He was scheduled to fly back to London later in the day, but it was only a matter of time before the story would break in the news, and I wanted him to hear what happened from us first.

"Hey, it's G," I said somberly, waiting for Leon to wake up.

"I know bad news travels when you call me at 3:00 a.m., girl. What's up?" he asked, half awake.

"Alana was in a car crash. She's gone," I said. There was a long pause as I waited for Leon to process that statement.

"What! I'm up, Gina. Talk." I heard things being knocked to the floor on the other end of the line.

I tried to explain what I knew, which wasn't a ton of information. Leon was already scheduled for the 12:00 p.m. flight from New York back to London, but he said he was going to head to JFK for the earlier flight and would come straight to my house when he landed. He swore he wouldn't say anything about Alana's passing to anyone yet. We were still waiting on information.

I went to check on Athene. She was sitting in the living room in tears, blaming herself for Alana's death and saying how she wished she had been nicer to her. I know she felt bad.

"I was so mean to her, Gina," she said, crying. I went over to Athene and held her, telling her it wasn't doing her any good to blame herself and that Rick and David needed her strength, not her weakness. I told her that I was going to call the hospital. As I headed for the phone, it rang. It was Sebastian.

"Babe, this is getting weird. I'm on my way home," Sebastian said before hanging up the phone.

Athene and I waited for Sebastian, who would be home in a few minutes. Ten minutes later, we heard Sebastian's car pull up the driveway and then heard him walking through the front door and into the library where we were sitting.

"David woke up. I got to see him. He has some scrapes and bruises, but the doctors can't say anything until they run more tests.

He's going to be in hospital for a few days. Rick is staying there to-night," Sebastian said, exhausted. He sat down and told us that the local police came and inquired about Alana's recent state of mind. The police said there wasn't another car involved in the accident that they could determine, based on the lack of tire marks on the road. It appeared she had plowed into a tree."

I got up and walked out of the room, heading to the guest bed-room. There I started crying. An hour later, at 2:00 a.m., Sebastian came into the bedroom, waking me up.

"Baby, you sleeping?"

I rolled over to face him but with my eyes closed. He wanted to talk, something he rarely ever wanted to do.

"I wish I'd never gone to get that shirt from Emily," he said, mad at himself for the decision he had made. I insisted that this was in no way his fault, but he began expressing guilt for all the things he'd done to hurt me in the past. He was feeling bad about all the negative words he'd ever spoken about Alana, too. Sebastian got into bed and told me how much he loved me and that he would never put me through anything like that, ever. Sebastian was pissed off at Rick but wondered if filing for divorce would have made things better or worse for Alana's state of mind. We were both profoundly sad, but the sadness was mixed with anger at her for trying to take her son's life along with hers. We were both confused and angry about her actions.

I got up many times during the night. I was restless after Sebastian came to bed, waking up haunted by the part I'd played in getting Alana to confess to Rick about speaking Greek. I was struggling with my own guilt, playing the scene out in my mind over and over.

At 8:30 a.m., the smell of coffee came wafting in from the kitchen. Sebastian's parents had stayed the night, and Athene was up making coffee and breakfast. I went into the kitchen, where Richard was sitting and waiting for Sebastian to go to hospital.

Facing the reality of a death in the family, together with the onslaught of new information about a possible suicide, left us all distraught and confused, each with our own guilty feelings about pushing Alana. I'd never realized that Alana was this fragile, and if I had, I would never have pushed her the way I had.

Alana and I were very different when it came to confrontation with our guys. Alana refused to confront Rick about his affairs on the road directly; instead, she dropped hints that she knew and accepted it as part of her life. Rick never brought home a stray, as she put it; he was faithful to her at home. But she knew he wasn't on the road. The last affair must have hit too close to home for her to deal with it. What was disturbing and unbelievably sad was that she could have just left him. She didn't need to end her life and plan to take David with her. It was an unbelievably selfish act.

Sebastian made his way downstairs, where he was met by a somber group that didn't have much to say to one another. Sebastian, pouring himself some coffee, told me he and his parents were going to go see Rick and David. He asked me to start notifying people that a funeral was to take place on Sunday and to start making the calls to his friends and business contacts. I somberly mentioned that Leon was arriving soon from New York and that he was staying on with us. Sebastian nodded his head in acknowledgement and changed the subject back to placing calls. He asked me to call Lacey first. She could make the news travel faster in the States. He said Chip and Marcus were leaving New York today and staying with us also. We were to have a full house.

Later in the day, after Sebastian and his parents left, Nigel came over as I was preparing tea. I saw him outside and invited him in. I wanted to explain the commotion that had be going on at the house, not mentioning my little trip to hospital. Nigel and I were in conversation when Leon came in the door and walked back into the kitchen.

"Come here, girl," Leon said, giving me a hug. "What can I do?" Leon asked. I looked over to Nigel and said that we needed to start calling the Tin Garden contacts. Nigel said he and Melba would be available for anything we needed. I took him up on it. I told him that we had a house full of people coming, and if Melba could go to the store, that would be really helpful. Nigel took a sip of tea and, leaving the cup on the counter, took off for his house to get Melba.

Leon had a look of disbelief, but we were both on the same page. We jumped into action mode. We knew what to do; we needed to make calls and minimize direct conversation with all people we needed to reach out to. Leon said he would call Joe and Andy.

"If I call them, the story will circle at least twice in the family network hotline, right?" Leon said. It was an accurate assessment.

Leon and I went outside to the recording studio, where Sebastian kept all his work-related documents and numbers. Looking at his desk, I found a three-ring binder with the word *wait* written on it in black marker. Inside were bills, receipts, tour diagrams, and riders. There was a call list folded in half near the back of the book. Leon and I made a copy of the list and cut it in half, discussing whether we should call Emily or not. There was no way for Emily not to hear about Alana's death, but I wasn't going to make that call. I wasn't taking sides. I didn't want to ice Emily out because of bad choices she and Rick made, but I'd rather not tell her myself out of respect for Alana. Family before business. Leon was in full agreement; we had to leave Emily off the call list.

As Leon and I were finishing up all the necessary calls, there was a knock on the door. Leon went to answer it. It was Chip and Marcus; they had just arrived from the States. The driver put the luggage in the foyer. Leon took the guys into the library bar and proceeded to make them cocktails. I asked Melba, who had just finished putting away groceries, if she could help me change the sheets in the guest bedrooms. She said she would handle it and told me to tend to my guests.

I walked over to Chip and Marcus, who I had not seen since the 'Wait Tour,' and gave them hugs. I asked Marcus where his girl-friend was.

"My girlfriend, Cindy, didn't know Alana. This is pretty damn strange, though, right?" Marcus said. I told them they didn't know the half of it. Leon came from around the back of the bar and handed them cocktails.

"So … Sebastian came home last night and said that the police had asked about Alana's state of mind," I said. Everyone raised their eyebrows.

"State of mind?" Leon repeated.

"Apparently, there was no other car involved. She hit a tree. No skid marks were found on the road," I said somberly.

"Are you saying she committed suicide, Gina?" Chip asked, confused.

"It appears that way, according to the police" I replied.

"Why in the fuck would she do that?" Marcus asked.

"Rick's affair got too close to home, perhaps," I replied, assuming that was the reason why.

"Did she find out Em's pregnant?" Chip asked as he took a sip of his drink and leaned into the back on the couch, spilling information we didn't know.

"What do you mean she's pregnant? Who told you that?" I asked Chip, sternly.

"Rick did, a week ago," Chip replied.

"Oh, this is a damn mess. Get the fuck out of here. And I work with that bitch, too," Leon said, shocked to hear the news.

"Rick told you Emily was pregnant?" I asked, really pissed off.

"Yeah, G. I thought Bas would have told you that," Chip replied.

"No, he didn't tell me that," I stated, really disappointed.

"Shit, I thought Bas would have told you," he said, embarrassed, as I got up and went into the guest room to pull out the baby dirty-dog T-shirt. I threw it at Chip.

"See this? Sebastian brought that home to me last night. You better spill whatever you have now," I demanded, really aggravated.

"Yeah, it's Bas's tour shirt. Looks small. And?" Chip said, looking at it confused.

"And you better start spilling it, Chip. Who got her pregnant?" I said, demanding an answer.

"Emily is saying Rick did. Hey, keep me out of it. I don't know," Chip replied, wanting to end the conversation.

"He has a child, Chip, one who, by the way, is in intensive care because she tried to take not just her own life but David's life too. Did you know that?" I said.

"Marcus and I only heard from Stan yesterday, G. I haven't talked to Bas or Rick yet. Stan's coming over, right?" Chip asked, trying to change the subject.

"Yes, he's staying in London with Lex. He'll be here tomorrow," I replied.

Sebastian walked in, having heard raised voices in the library. He went over and greeted his band mates, hugging them. Leon was looking at me pensively, wanting to talk. I grabbed Leon and brought him upstairs as Melba was coming down the stairs with laundry in her hands.

"We need to talk," I said as I invited Leon in and shut the door. I needed to tell Leon about my baby news fast before he heard it from Sebastian.

"No shit, we need to talk," Leon replied, taken aback by the events unfolding.

"Leon, first, I have news I need to tell you," I said firmly.

"What? You gonna tell me you're pregnant too?" Leon said.

I paused and looked down. Then I took Leon's hand, looked him in the eyes, and shook my head yes. Leon let out a scream that could be heard downstairs. Sebastian yelled back, asking what was wrong. I told Leon to stay quiet as I opened the door, yelling back to Sebastian that nothing was wrong and shutting the door abruptly to continue my conversation with Leon.

"Damn, girl, you both be pregnant at the same time? That bitch done stole your thunder, Gina," Leon said in a lowered voice. He was really aggravated with the news about Emily. "Does Bridgette know about this yet?"

I shook my head no. I told Leon that he was the first to know, because I was having some problems and didn't want to tell them right away.

"You're our damn sister. You can't be keeping this kind of shit … We're tighter than that, girl," Leon said, disappointed that I had not told him sooner.

I explained to Leon that I'd had some issues with bleeding but that it had stopped.

"This is too much. I can't take this in, Gina. You got death, new babies, complications. My head is spinin. I need another drink," Leon said as he stormed out of the room and headed downstairs to make a cocktail. He marched behind the bar, picked up a glass, and started throwing ice cubes in it, interrupting Sebastian's conversation with Chip and Marcus. That's when Leon decided to take it to the street with Sebastian.

"Oh, congratulations, Sebastian. Appears your pecker works. I was concerned it wouldn't. What secrets are you holding? Care to share?" Leon said, sassy, looking over at Sebastian and taking a sip of his cocktail.

"What do you mean, Leon?" Sebastian replied with an odd look. Everyone in the room went silent, except for Leon.

"You and I had an understanding in Greece, my man. I guess I'll be getting the call for the dual baby shower, not to mention the Greek food prepared by your mother. She'll be over the moon to help with that shit. Doesn't seem fair to Gina, who would like to bask in that baby joy by herself, considering all she's been through with your ass," Leon said with an attitude.

"Are you talking about Emily being knocked up? I don't know if that's Rick's kid," Sebastian said dismissively with an aggravated tone.

"Is it yours, Sebastian? Em isn't fucking anyone other than Roland boys. I'm not the bitch you want to play with today. I'm not in the mood," Leon said as he rolled his eyes at Sebastian.

"Fuck no, it's not mine, and I don't want Gina involved in this bullshit," Sebastian replied with anger in his voice.

"I'm not doing Roland-boy drama again. I swear on the fall line of Louis Vuitton, if Gina ever sheds one tear to me that isn't about baby joy or how much she loves your ass … me and you, we will have some problems. I'm over the shit Sebastian," Leon said. He turned around and walked back to the bar, slamming down his glass.

"I never had sex with Emily, Leon," Sebastian replied with an awkward smirk.

"But you knew about her and Rick, and that's really bad. You feel me?" Leon said, raising his voice.

"Leon, I'll never hurt G. You know that," Sebastian replied, trying to dismiss the conversation.

"No, Sebastian, you already did that, and everyone in this room knows it," Leon said, getting more aggravated.

"This is really old shit, Leon. She told you she's having problems, right?" Sebastian replied, looking directly at Leon. Chip and Marcus were sitting on the couch, somewhat entertained by the discussion.

"Don't change the subject, Sebastian. I'm not the bitch you want to fuck with today! You keeping shit like this from Gina makes you look guilty! Don't get me started with Alana ... I'll wait on that," Leon said, making himself another drink,

Chip, Marcus, and I were watching them go at it. Leon had on his angry-queen hat, and he wasn't sipping tea. He was drinking several Manhattans and reading Sebastian's tea leaves. Listening to their come-to-Jesus session proved to me that Sebastian was still covering for Rick, and it all tied back again to Chip, who covers for the both of them.

I interrupted and asked Sebastian how long he'd known about Emily being pregnant. He replied that he'd only known a few days, and that's why he'd gone to see Emily in the first place. He'd chosen not to tell me yet because he didn't want me upset. Emily had told Rick she was three months pregnant, and the news was now spilling all over the Roland library bar. Sebastian was aggravated with Leon for bringing up his brother and Emily, and the whole argument between them started again.

"This is why I didn't tell her. You think I don't care? That's crazy, Leon," Sebastian snapped.

"I didn't say you didn't care; what I said was that you didn't care enough to tell your wife your brother got his mistress pregnant! What, you didn't think she would find out? Boy, please," Leon said making another cocktail.

"He's my brother, Leon!" Sebastian replied, angered.

"And Gina's my sister ... And?" Leon retorted, starring Sebastian down.

"And I'm not taking sides, Leon. It's a fucked-up situation, and it pisses me off," Sebastian replied.

"It's not about taking sides. The Roland boys get caught in nasty business, and I'm going to be listening to Rick's baby mama cry, bitch, and cry for the next six months. Let me be clear with you … I'm not doing the Roland boy drama again. You and I had the talk, Sebastian," Leon said, staring at him.

Leon and Sebastian's discussion went on for several minutes. I got up and left the room, and Marcus and Chip followed behind me. I told them I was going to order Chinese takeaway, and both of them offered to pick it up so they could get away from the heated conversation.

I was waiting in the kitchen for Chip and Marcus to come back with the food, when Leon and Sebastian walked in, having just finished their discussion. They gave each other a hug, making up. Leon's issues with Sebastian had built up over time. Their conversation had nothing to do with Sebastian withholding information from me. Leon was angry about the Emily issue because he was now circled in the drama by default.

Chip and Marcus came back with food, and everyone grabbed a plate and sat down. Marcus asked Leon if that was his first "Wait" meltdown, chuckling as he asked. He told him that it was a normal process, coming off a crazy tour where you worked and lived with eleven other people on a bus—the afterburn left from the four-week crazies, as he put it. One day, for no reason, you remember that someone pissed you off months ago and then snap on that person a year later.

"Very normal after a tour; don't feel bad, Leon," Marcus said, laughing.

Chip explained to Leon that if he and I would have stuck around for the entire tour, we would've witnessed a full-band meltdown that happened on stage, with Sebastian throwing his microphone at Stan, hitting him in the head, after an encore song and Marcus hurling drumsticks at Rick for calling him a jackass on stage. Leon asked Chip what his meltdown had been about. Chip paused and replied with a chuckle, "I snapped at Lacey, but she got me back by putting honey and sugar all over my bass amp."

"What did you do to her?" Leon asked.

"I told her that I was sending her back to Joe with a fuck-you card after the tour was over," Chip replied with a misogynistic attitude.

"Oh, I would have done more to you than that. Lacey is a cool girl, Chip," Leon said, raising his eyebrow.

"I know. I felt bad, but that sugar shit was messed up. A week later she sent me a fuck-off card. I made the mistake of calling her and saying, "That's all you got?" The next day she left a pile of dog shit at my door," Chip replied with a cocky laugh.

"You had that coming, Chip." Sebastian said as he started laughing.

"Yeah. Fuck, I shouldn't have hit that; she lives too close to me," Chip replied, laughing.

"You were being a dick, my friend." Sebastian replied, casually laughing.

The post-tour banter went around the table while everyone was finishing their dinner. Sebastian suggested to the guys that they go pay Rick and David a visit at hospital. After they left, Leon and I made a call to Bridgette so I could tell her that I was pregnant and that I was having some slight difficulties. Bridgette said she was coming for the funeral and would be arriving on Sunday.

Funeral for a Friend

Everyone was getting ready to leave our house for Alana's funeral. Sebastian, Leon, and I took my car, and Chip and Marcus took Sebastian's. When we arrived at the cemetery, we saw she had one living family member in attendance, an uncle named Martin. Alana's parents had passed away before she and Rick had met.

David had been released from hospital the day before, and I wasn't sure how I felt about him attending his own mother's funeral. The experience was hard enough for adults. I figured that this would haunt David for the rest of his life and that he would struggle with issues about it later. We were all reminded of how short life was by the bruises and cuts on David's little face. It was an incredibly sad day. Sebastian had David in his arms for most of the service. He was holding on to Sebastian, crying and not understanding what was going on, only that mommy was in heaven. It broke my heart.

Sebastian got up and took David away before they lowered Alana's coffin into the dirt to minimize the trauma. He walked toward the parked cars. I sat through the service next to Leon and Bridgette, who had just arrived in London that morning. Bridgette had started her London-to-Milan route a few days prior and had not established her new crash pad yet. Bridgette and Leon were making plans to get a flat (apartment) together in a few weeks. They talked after the services ended about how the Christopher Street Gang would need to be re-named once they found their new place. Leon made the comment that somehow *Christopher Street* sounded better than *Bath Road*, which was the location Leon and Bridgette were leaning toward.

Leon, Bridgette, and I then spoke to Alana's uncle Martin. He told us about Alana's mother, who had passed when she was a child, and how Alana had never known her. What shocked me was that he said this was his curse, losing women in his life, and he hoped the curse would end with him and not transfer on to David. His statement was profoundly sad, and his pain was indescribable. I felt empathy for Martin, having some knowledge that Alana's death was probably suicide. I felt like I was covering for Rick like Sebastian had done so many times before. I had gotten my first realistic dose of what Sebastian dealt with. It was more than a messed-up situation; it was dirty business. Rick would face his reality every day when he looked into David's eyes.

After we left the cemetery, everyone came over to our house for food and drinks. Mansion Roland always had people coming in and out, and I was growing tired of the drama quickly. My mood was picked up by the guests when I decided to go upstairs to lay down, leaving Sebastian to deal with everyone. I had no more bandwidth to deal with drama, his parents, his brother, and all of them. I wanted a retreat to be by myself, even without Sebastian. I wasn't upstairs for more than ten minutes before Sebastian came up to the bedroom.

"Baby, are you feeling okay?" he asked as I gave him a look that said it was probably not a good time to be talking to me right now.

"I'm fine, Sebastian. Please just leave me alone," I replied as I turned over on the bed with my back to him.

"Gina, seriously, are you feeling okay?" he insisted.

"Please go and leave me alone," I said, not looking at him.

"Gina, if you're not feeling well, I'll have everyone leave right now," he replied.

"No, Sebastian, please just go to them. I have no more energy for these lies," I stated with tears in my eyes.

"What do you mean, Gina?" Sebastian asked somberly?

"We're now covering for Rick and his bullshit," I replied, wiping the tears from my eyes.

"Gina, I don't want you involved in this mess. I told you that," he replied.

"I don't want you involved in it either, Sebastian. It makes me sick," I said.

Sebastian came over to the bed and lay down next to me, putting his arm over my hip and placing his hand on my stomach. "I love you, Gina. My brother cheated, yes, but it wasn't always like that. Alana was on medication for depression. You don't know what Rick has been through with her," he said.

"You're right, Sebastian, I don't know, because you never tell me anything. I'm over all the lies and secrets. If you can't talk to me, why are we even together? Am I just being used as a baby machine to pump out your kids?" I said, mad.

"Is that what you think?" Sebastian said, disappointed in my comment.

"Answer the question with some honesty: did you marry me because I fit the bill of the nice girl, not the town whore, to have kids with?" I asked.

"That is a seriously fucked-up thing to say to me, Gina. Is this a hormonal thing you're going through?" he asked me.

"No, Sebastian, it's a someone-died-because-of-the-lies thing that has me in a mood. Please forgive me for not being a doting housewife for a few hours. Now, can you leave me alone?" I demanded.

Sebastian got up. I could tell he was really hurt by what I had said to him. I was confused over a senseless death. I wasn't able to process it. I had guilt and anger issues I was dealing with myself.

Sebastian waited a few minutes and then sent Bridgette upstairs to talk to me. Bridgette and I spoke about my pregnancy, the funeral, and Rick. I was moody and ultrasensitive to Bridgette's comments, which I would normally let roll off my back.

"Sebastian is not the issue here, Gina. You know that I'd have no problem telling you he was if I thought so. Don't push him away because of Rick's bullshit. You need to stand by your man, Gina, the man *you* picked, sister-friend," Bridget said.

"I picked? Seriously, Bridgette? No, that's not what happened. The universe decided that I needed to deal with a pill-popping drug addict to have a kid with. I didn't seek to fall in love with him, Bridgette. He found me in Greece. I didn't look for him; I went there to get over him," I replied with an attitude.

"He found you because he loves you, Gina. I was never a fan of this man, but he has changed. Rick's bullshit is not his problem. I see this now. His brother is the one who's fucked up, and Sebastian follows and cleans up after him. I'm sorry I was ever that hard on him. He is one of the good ones, Gina," Bridgette said.

I wanted to end the Sebastian conversation. "Don't make him out to be a saint. He has done some shit to me," I replied.

"And you let him, Gina. Don't forget that. You let that shit happen. Get up and come downstairs. Stop the fucking pity party. You need to go an apologize to him now," Bridgette replied, aggravated.

Bridgette and I went downstairs, and I walked over to Sebastian to tell him how sorry I was for saying what I did. He understood and said that having all the people in the house post-funeral was too much for me to handle. Bridgette and Leon were staying on with us, along with Marcus and Chip. Sebastian told them he was taking me upstairs and going to bed.

Sebastian pulled back the covers and slid in next to me, pulling me into him when he did. "I want to make love to you," he said as he placed his hand behind my neck, pulling me closer to him. "I'm sorry, Gina. After Lex and I are finished next week, you and I should get out of town."

"Where are we running to?" I asked, surprised.

"We're not running, G. Might be nice just to get out of town," he said as he entered me. It had been about a week since we had made love. Then, after two minutes, he said, "Baby, you feel really good. I'm not going to last." I was surprised he came that fast and told him that I needed a redo. "You're tight. I won't last, G, but you'll need to wait so I can reload. I should have gone down on you first."

"So … go ahead," I replied.

"I just came inside of you," he said in a pointed tone.

"So?" I replied flippantly.

"That has to come first, baby. Sorry … You have an eat-out-free coupon waiting for you," he said, laughing.

"Fine, I'll hold that blow-job coupon until after I use mine," I replied.

"You used to hate me going down on you. What changed your mind?" he asked.

"When you took your time doing it on our honeymoon," I replied.

"I brought my A game that night. I'm functioning on a half tank right now," he said.

"Our sex life used to be amazing. Now I'm lucky when I get it at all," I replied.

"I can't do it every night of the week until 3:00 a.m.," he said, raising his eyebrow.

"We used to do that all the time, Sebastian," I replied in a disappointed tone.

"We used to fuck, G. Making love is different than fucking. We've been down this road," he replied in a dismissive tone.

"So I was just a fuck?" I asked in disbelief.

"When I met you, yes, Gina, we were fucking," he replied, circling around the question and making a point not to piss me off.

"Oh, I see. Well, I never had casual sex with you, Sebastian," I stated.

"I know, because you were in love with me from, like, day two," he replied.

"I'll remember that comment the next time you want a blow job," I replied.

"Threating to hold out on a blow job isn't going to make this conversation better. It's only going to piss me off," he replied.

"You're holding out on me … so what's the difference?" I asked.

"There is a big difference, Gina. I'm having an honest conversation with you. I have a history of going off the reservation; keep that in mind," he stated.

"Don't threaten me about getting it someplace else. I don't deserve that. If you want an open conversation about not being faithful in this marriage, then by all means, fire away. I won't judge you," I stated.

"I have tail thrown at me. The temptation is there, Gina. I'm a man; it means nothing to me if a girl wants to suck my dick. But for you, it means the sky is falling," he replied with a nonchalant, rock-star, jackass attitude.

"Where you put your dick matters to me," I replied.

"If a girl wants to put it in her mouth and suck me off, it's kind of hard to say no. Doesn't mean I'm going to stick it in her. I wouldn't do that to you Gina," he said.

"Okay, let's say some guy put his dick in my mouth. How does that sound to you?" I asked, knowing what his answer would be.

"That would make you a whore," he stated angrily.

"Okay, so you let whores suck you off?" I asked.

"I'll let a whore suck me off. I can't fall in love with a whore, Gina," he replied.

"So did you see me as a whore when we met?" I asked.

"No, Gina, but I wasn't in love with you when we first got together. It took a while to get to that," he replied.

"Why?" I asked.

"Fuck, G! Because no man falls in love that fast. Jesus Christ. I would've been fine having a kid with you without ever getting married again, but you deserved more than that," he stated, angry.

"Well at least you're honest," I replied.

"That attitude right there makes me want to share more with you," he said sarcastically.

"So what does that mean?" I asked.

"That means I love you and I will try to keep my dick out of a whore's mouth next time I'm out on tour," he said like a complete rock-star asshole.

"Oh, I see. Just on tour, Sebastian?" I asked.

"Come on, Gina. I'm not going to fuck other girls. Blow jobs, maybe," he replied with a snicker, thinking he was being cute.

"You like to put your dick into things and come home later wagging your tail. I'll make an appointment with the vet next Tuesday," I replied, not engaging further in the discussion.

"Come on, Gina, I was kidding," he replied.

It wasn't the right time for me to have this very frank, open and honest conversation about keeping his dick in his pants and out of some groupie's mouth. He didn't see blow jobs as cheating, and that was a huge problem with this group of guys in general. He was trying to plant the seed in my head of the possibility of future tour blow jobs, trying to change my thought process on the free fuck pass. What he didn't realize was, two could play at that game. My singing days may have been over, but my tour days were just getting started. I was about to start a new Roland family tradition; his child would be joining him on tour. Try getting a blow job while you're holding your kid in your arms. Not going to happen, jackass.

Lei Dorme, the Rock Opera

It had been a few months since Alana's funeral. Lex and Sebastian had finished working on the rock opera *Lei Dorme*. The cast had been selected, and the orchestra was in place. It was the week before opening night, and Lex had asked Tin Garden to perform a special one-off show for industry insiders to showcase the new arrangements with the orchestra. They were also going to be recording an album that evening. I had been asked by Lex to do my swan song number for this one and only performance with Tin Garden. I had said in the past that I would never perform the song again, however I did it at Lex's request. To deny a request from Lex was not an act of friendship; it would have been considered an act of betrayal.

The show had been sold out for weeks, and the guys were not entertaining the idea of adding a second performance. Tin Garden decided to give their audience just enough not to lose their rock dignity to the world of cheesy rock operas

Sebastian and I arrived at the theatre with Marcus and Chip. Rick was already there. I was a bit taken aback when I saw that he was with Emily, so soon after the death of his wife. I didn't address either one of them right away. Instead, I went over to say hello to Lex and Carl, who were off bickering in a corner.

"Gina, my dear, you look beautiful," Lex said, breaking away from Carl and giving me a kiss on the cheek hello. I asked what they were bickering about.

"Carl seems to think that Marcus is gay," Lex said.

I started laughing. "No ... Marcus has a girlfriend you know that," I replied, with a smile. Carl knew that Marcus had a girlfriend in New York. Carl liked him though.

"Carl was doing some basket shopping earlier," Lex said, looking over at Carl.

"You're such an old Grimm's fairy," Carl snapped back at Lex.

"That's Mother Superior to you," Lex replied in a dignified manner as Carl walked away. If these two were not bickering, then you could assume there was a real problem.

Lex and I walked over to join Sebastian and Rick. Standing there, I noticed Emily had gone over to the other side of the room and was speaking to Leon and Bridgette. I excused myself from Sebastian and Lex to join them. Sebastian thought it was a good idea for me to clear the air and play nice with Emily. I hadn't spoken to her since the tour, but I anticipated that the conversation was going to be awkward. What could I say? Hey, great news, we're going to have kids the same age? No.

"Hello, Emily," I said, looking at her, as Bridgette and Leon surveyed our reactions to one another.

"Hello, Gina, and before you say anything to me, I'm in love with him, so back the bus up," Emily said defensively.

"Can't find your own slang to use? Took that from him too?" I said, hitting her with the truth.

"Gina, Rick is my guy, so get use to the idea," she said in a snarky tone.

"Why are you so defensive, Emily?" I asked.

"Because you're not the only one carrying precious cargo, Gina," she replied.

"Precious cargo? Where have I heard that before? Oh yeah, from Sebastian, who actually *asked* me to have his baby," I replied with major attitude.

"How do you know Rick didn't ask me to have his?" Emily retorted.

"Seriously, Emily? It's too bad you've had this thing about me since we ran in the same circle. Have a nice night," I said, and I walked away. I did kind of expect to get this attitude from her. I was never a fan of the Stitch Bitch; she got her nickname for a reason. I had tried many times to be friendly toward her on tour, but she was a bitch to me from the word go. My perception of Emily was that she saw people as beneath her. Emily had a successful rock-and-roll clothing line, and rock stars were into her stuff. She was very talented in that respect.

But she'd trapped Rick with a baby, trying to win his affection, when she wasn't able to trap Sebastian.

I went back to let Sebastian know that the conversation didn't go well, and he said we could talk about it later. Bridget walked over, and we headed off to Tin Garden's dressing room.

"She is a bitch, Gina," Bridgette said as she shut the door. Leon came in a few minutes later, embarrassed.

"I told Emily that she wasn't correct in her attitude toward you and that she needed to apologize. Don't expect that to come from her anytime soon," Leon said.

"What is her deal?" Bridgette asked.

Leon explained to Bridgette that Emily perceived me as the biggest threat to her position. Leon told us he and Emily were working on fonts for her new embossed stationery, which would give her name as Emily Ann Roland, and she'd told Leon she was going to start a new children's rock-and-roll clothing line called Hear, a play on her new initials. Emily was moving forward, taking Rick's last name prematurely. Well, at least her soon-to-be child would have it anyway

It was time for Tin Garden to hit the stage for their one and only night performance of this rock opera. After about an hour, Lex came to get me for my number.

"Gina, my, how things turn around. You look radiant, dear," Lex said.

"Funny how a pair of boots and a chance meeting got me here," I replied.

"Gina, your determination to study and unwavering spirit got you here," Lex said.

"Lex, when you taught me this song, I never thought I would be standing in front of more than ten people singing it," I replied.

"Gina, this is your song because Sebastian made it so. Reach down and find that pain again, and you'll connect with your audience. The greatest gift they can give you, if you accept it, will be the applause that you so greatly deserve. Are you ready, my dear?" Lex said as he took my hand and led me to the stage.

When Lex and I approached, the guys were waiting to go back

out after the intermission. Tin Garden was taking the stage after me as I was the headliner of this number. Funny how life turns around.

As I stood waiting to go out, I thought about how my entire professional career had never that moment where I got to connect with an audience by myself. The closest I'd ever come to that was with Q McGovern when we went rogue doing Jingle and Belles. I turned to Sebastian. This would be the last time I would ever be able to connect with an audience. Sebastian paused and looked at me as the other guys took the stage.

Lex leaned in close to my ear and said, "If he left you and your baby, Gina, how would that feel?" And right then, tears started welling up in my eyes. Sebastian, took to the stage, and I waited until the cue from Lex. I was pretty far along in my pregnancy and was emotional anyway, but I was determined to recapture some of that raw emotion I'd had in DC as I walked onto the stage.

As I walked across the stage, the sequins on my dress were sparkling in the overhead stage lights, creating sunburst patterns on the black stage floor. The beautiful, black, long dress hid my baby bump. I looked over to Sebastian and then addressed the audience as cheers echoed through the theater.

"Thank you … I made a statement long ago that I would never perform this song again. Well … here I am. This song holds special meaning for me in many ways. I hope you enjoy it. This is … 'Lei Dorme.'" The audience gave a round of loud applause, and the orchestra started playing. As I waited for the strings to start and listened to the sound of Rick's guitar, an image from that fateful night in DC came back to me. I glanced over at Sebastian, who was sitting at the piano. I had become overwhelmed with emotion at Lex's mention of Sebastian leaving me. As I sang "In your heart a secret lies; what my pain is, no one knows," I turned away from Sebastian, looking out at the audience. Tears started flowing down my face, and the audience was praising me.

After the song finished, I walked to the front of the stage and bowed, listening to the thunderous applause of the standing ovation that followed my song. I placed my hands to my heart and thanked the audience, taking in the sounds and finally accepting the appreciation of my singing abilities. Sebastian got up from the piano, and Rick and Chip came over, putting their hands on my back. Rick looked at Sebastian nervously and said, "We should have figured out an encore."

"In theater, we don't do encores. It's okay," I said into Rick's ear before waving to the audience and leaving the stage. Lex stopped me at stage left and turned me around to go back out and take one final bow with Tin Garden. I walked back on stage, waving to the audience. They were standing on their feet, cheering. It was an incredible feeling to have before leaving for the last time, knowing that my professional singing career was officially over. I was able to rewrite my own ending to "Lei Dorme," and no one could take that from me, not even the Stitch Bitch.

The Book of Sebastian

October 1987 was the highlight of my life. Gina and I were looking forward to welcoming our baby. We had just come back from the ultrasound, where we'd found out we were a having a boy. In the car on the way back home, Gina said she wanted to change the baby's name again.

"What about Adonis Sebastian?" Gina asked.

"Baby, it'd be nice to have Richard as his middle name after my dad," I replied.

"Or we can call him Zeus," she said, serious.

"Zeus? Fuck no, Gina," I replied.

"Adonis Zeus?" she asked.

"It doesn't work like that, Gina. You and my mom with the *Zeus*. Fuck," I said, annoyed because Gina and my mother were into the Zeus crap.

"We could call him Z," Gina said.

"No, Gina!" I declared. "End of discussion."

When it came to this Greek shit going off the rails, I blamed my mother. Right after we found out the sex of the baby, my mom, Bridgette, and Leon gave Gina a baby shower at our house. The day of the shower, I came downstairs and walked into the kitchen to find my mom sticking Greek flag toothpicks in appetizers. When I asked her what that was about, she told me to go and check if we had enough ice for the party. I went to the bar to see if they had ice and instead found a bowl of cocktail stir sticks with Greek gods on the ends of them. As I stood holding one, Nigel came inside and asked me if he could park the guests' cars when they arrived to keep them off the lawn. Nigel and I went outside, and that's when I saw Bridgette hanging an Olympic flag on the side of my house. Seeing that, I went back inside, stopping at the bar to grab the bowl of cocktail stirrers with Zeus and friends, and went to my mom.

"What's up with the Olympic flag and this shit?" My mom told me to leave her be, to stay out of the way, and not to ask questions.

I hung back in the kitchen. I wanted to see where the day was headed. After the guests arrived, Leon started a game where they went through a list of Greek gods to guess the name of the baby, giving clues and shit like that. But it all took a dive when the guests were asked to go outside for an Olympic javelin diaper throw in the front yard. Bridgette had cloth diapers with apples in them for weight, and the guests would see how far they could toss them to win a prize. It was pretty damn ridiculous. Nigel and I were outside watching this crap in disbelief, and after everyone left, he was on the ladder, pulling diapers out of the trees.

A few days after the baby shower, I started finding little Greek statues and shit all over our fucking house. Gina was in the kitchen with my mom and Bridgette talking and being overly animated about painting the baby's room with a scene of Athens. I overheard this in the downstairs bathroom while I was taking a leak. I glanced over at the mirror and saw the reflection of a Poseidon painting that was hanging on the wall, which scared the shit out of me. I turned around, took the damn thing off the wall, walked by them with it in my hand, and put it outside in the trash can. I had reached my limit of all fucking things Greek.

I came back inside, where the hens were now siting in silence, and looked over at Gina. "You lost your Greek god privileges. I don't want to hear it. Oh, and mom … don't speak Greek to me for a month," I said, walking past them, going upstairs, and slamming the bedroom door. I may be half Greek, but fuck, that shit was annoying.

Several weeks later, I was laying down on the bed watching a Manchester United game when Gina came walking out of the bathroom.

"Sebastian, I think it's time," she said as Norman Whiteside was taking it in for a goal. "Sebastian, I think I'm having the baby." She stood looking at me to get up.

"Baby? Baby, oh shit, now?" I replied, torn between having my kid and having Norman take it to the goal again. I jumped out of bed and grabbed her bag by the door, and off we went to the hospital.

In the car, Gina was saying she was in pain, and I needed to keep her relaxed.

"This will be over soon," I said, holding her hand and trying to shift.

"Hurry, Sebastian, the pain is getting worse," she said, trying to get comfortable.

"Okay, G, just relax. We are almost there," I said as I pulled onto the street of Royal Hospital.

"Sebastian, I'm so scared," she said with tears starting to form in her eyes.

"Gina, baby, I'm going to be there the entire time. Don't be scared," I said as I pulled up to the entrance. I flagged down an intake person, who brought out a wheelchair to take her inside. I parked the car, and when I got in the front door, I was taken to a room where they scrubbed me up and put me in a doctor's gown. Then they shuffled me to a room where she was being prepped to have our baby.

Gina was in labor for about four hours, and during labor, she only called me a fucking asshole three times. After several hours and the final push, I heard the first cry of our child. Adonis came into our world on December 1. The nurse handed Gina our baby, and she looked over at me with the largest smile.

"This is your son, Sebastian," she said with tears in her eyes, and she handed him to me to hold. He was the most precious thing I had ever held in my hands—my son, my very own son. I loved this girl more than anything.

Gina was in the hospital for a few days after she had Adonis. She was weak from the anemia and was put on a IV drip for the rest of her time there. She wanted to breast feed our baby but couldn't. I moved into her room to stay with her, spending that time changing, feeding, and taking care of Adonis. Me and that kid bonded.

The day Gina was being released, I had Nigel go and pick up the new car I'd bought—a Rover—from the dealer. I ran back home to get it. Nigel and I tried to figure out how to put the car seat in, but Melba, seeing us struggling with it, came over and did it herself in like two minutes. I headed back to the hospital to pick them up. When I got to Gina's room, she had Adonis ready to go and was all mouth and full of attitude. In the car, she complained about the baby weight that she hadn't magically lost.

"Gina, you just had a baby. Give yourself a break," I said.

"It's because of your dick I got this way. You need to screw this weight off of me," Gina replied angrily.

"Gina, we can't have sex for six weeks," I said.

"I hope you still want to have sex with me after all of this." Gina said.

Gina had it in her mind that I would find someone to replace her. She couldn't be replaced, but I got it. I hadn't given her much of a reason in the past to trust me. When we were dating, I was fucked up and didn't care about myself or anyone else. This girl loved me like no other. She'd given me a son, and I wanted to do something for her. Gina wasn't into material things. She liked simple shit. Cards, letters, anything I hand wrote to her she kept. Expensive shit I bought for her ended up in Leon's closet, sooner or later. She wasn't like most women. My Gina was different. I wrote a letter to my little punk rock girl to thank her for bringing our son into the world.

> To the love of my life:
>
> Because of you, I want to be a better person. We're two souls that found each other and created a beautiful son we called Adonis. You brought him into the world so that I could show him how to be a good man by loving his mommy first.
>
> Gina, if you don't already know it, let me say it again: I love you more than a really good blow job, and that's saying something.
>
> Guess who loves you? Your Greek-god, rock-star jackass.
>
> Only yours,
>
> Sebastian.

Gina liked my funny cards; those ended up on our bedroom mirror. The romantic ones she put in a box, saving them for Adonis. On the nights I worked late in the studio, I would come upstairs and find the box she kept those letters in lying next to our bed. She read them every day. I never said anything to her about it. I would just look at her, smile, and fall in love with her a little more each day.

The first week we had Adonis at home, it was a trial by fire. We were getting up to change and feed him every few hours. Gina was so good with him. To say she was a great mom would be an understatement. If Adonis started crying, she was the first one up. G always had Adonis in her arms, singing and talking to him like a young man, never speaking to him like a baby.

A few days before Christmas, Bridgette and Leon came to the house for the first time since Gina had come home. "I'm going to be your godmother," Bridgette said, holding Adonis.

Leon wasn't sure what to do as he surveyed Bridgette holding Adonis. "And I'm your fabulous, well-put-together Uncle Leon. I'm going to teach you how to read a tea leaf or two, child," Leon said.

"Do you want to hold your little man, Leon?" Gina asked, looking over at Leon.

"Girl, you know babies aren't my thing. But since I am going to be this child's godfather, we need to get bonding," Leon said, taking Adonis into his arms. Everyone was awestruck watching him hold our baby. "This child is rock-and-roll royalty. Oh, girl, it's like I'm holding a member of the royal family and shit." Leon laughed. Adonis put his little arms out to Leon's face. "Sebastian, this child looks like you. Lord, we're going to have two of you running around? Need to put you in check right fast, my little man."

Watching Leon bond with Adonis was funny, but we all knew that Leon was using humor at my expense to mask his true feelings. Leon was a solid dude. Gina had great friends who had her back. It was the right thing to have Bridgette and Leon be the godparents. It should have been Alana and Rick, but things were different now. Alana was gone, and Rick was fucked up. I agreed to this arrangement because Rick and Emily had had their baby girl Amelia in November.

Emily had iced out Gina when it came time for her baby shower, and G heard about it from Leon. Gina came crying to me that she wasn't invited, and it pissed me off. I'd had enough, and I told Rick to get Em in line before I did. Emily had always thought she was the lead bitch of Tin Garden.

This friction between her and Gina came to a head at a fashion event. Gina had gone to support L. T., Leon's new clothing line, and she went backstage to tell him how great his show was. Emily saw Gina go backstage and told G she needed to leave the area. She did, but in tears. Then she came home and told me about it. I decided it was time for me to shut down this shit with Em. I made a call to Joe from Raiders.

"Hey, it's Bas. I promoted Em to Stitch Cunt. Spin that one around the block. Let's see how fast it gets back." Emily called me an hour later bitching about being called a cunt. "Keep trying me, Em," I said, pissed off. Then I hung up on her.

My mom was really mad at Rick for getting into another knock-'em-up situation. He and Alana had gotten married when she was pregnant with David, but they were at least dating at the time, so it wasn't that earth shattering. But this time, Rick had been in a sex-only situation with Emily when he got her pregnant. I wasn't surprised he was looking for a way out of his situation. I knew he and Emily weren't going to work long term. Em was a nut case, Rick's typical type, but Rick had broken the rules of engagement on tour. Rick was married. I was in the process of getting divorced when I met Gina. Different rules of engagement.

Touring is a strange thing. You meet people who occupy your time on the road, and when the tour is over, you part ways until the next tour. But Rick and Emily had a long-term tour thing that carried over to home. The rules of engagement are don't sleep with the people from your hometown and don't shit where you eat if you're married. Rick fucked up and taught me a lesson about where I hang my hat on the road. No easy piece of ass was worth the fucking aggravation. I had my son, and he was the single most important person in my life next to Gina. I grew up after Adonis came into the world.

Tin Garden—New Album

It was the summer of 1988, and Tin Garden was back in the studio. We were working on our next album. I was the one who was usually tasked with writing the lyrics for our songs, but for the first time, all of us contributed to the writing process. I didn't have the headspace for writing about being depressed anymore, because I wasn't.

We'd locked ourselves away in my home studio for a solid month to finish the album and were near the end of recording our rough tracks. On the last day of recording, Chip and I began bouncing ideas off each other about what to call the new album. We had a few songs to play off of, but the title wasn't standing out. Rick walked into the studio without acknowledging us. He was bitching to himself about Em being an evil witch as he walked by, throwing his bag of shit on the floor. This was nothing new; it was pretty much Rick's daily mantra.

Marcus snickered and asked me, "How are Em and Rick getting along these days?"

"It's fucked," I replied.

Marcus started laughing, and Chip got a smile on his face.

"I think we just found the title for our new album. We can slap out a one-minute intro song called 'Fucked' and punk it up," Chip said, as Rick left the studio and headed to my house to use the phone. After Rick left, Chip started slapping a punk beat on his bass, singing "When something is beyond repair, it's fucked. How's your life? It's fucked ..." Chip wrote the entire "Fucked" song in five minutes. Marcus and I were dying laughing as I put Chip in the iso booth. I grabbed my guitar, Marcus got on the drums, and we recorded it.

"When something is beyond repair, it's fucked. When good things go bad, it's fucked. It's fucked to be fucked over; it's fucked. Wrap it up so you don't get fucked," Chip sang, trying to keep a straight face. We were laughing for an hour.

Rick came back as we were finishing the song and found us on the floor, laughing our asses off. When we mentioned the new title for the next album to Rick, he wasn't exactly on board with having an album called "Fucked." He claimed it would have no commercial value. Marcus, Chip, and I took the other side of the argument. We thought it would be interesting to see what the radio stations would actually call the album, assuming it would be referred to as the *F* album.

Chip and I, from the beginning, wanted to get back to the basics and cut our teeth on something we hadn't done before. The music industry was changing and was oversaturated with bubblegum pop and hair metal. We needed to dumb our shit down, make it really simple. We were a rock band with a drummer who added an extra dimension to our overall sound, a guitar player who was well accomplished, a bass player heavily influenced by punk music, and a front man who still had a few more tricks left in him.

I observed Rick and Marcus having a conversation in the corner of the room. They were making plans for the next tour, talking about leasing a private jet and wondering if the jet company would let us paint *The Fucked Tour* on the side of the plane. Rick knew you could paint whatever you wanted on the side of a jet you were leasing, even if it was in bad taste, but I had no intention of chiming in on their convo. I was in a different phase of my life now.

Rick was always the driving force behind us putting out a new album. This had to do with his fucked choices in relationships, hence the song. Touring for him was a distraction from his home issues. Touring for me had been an escape vehicle to overindulge in drugs and alcohol. Rick could've lived his life out on the road 365 days a year if he didn't have kids. I hated touring, and the guys knew it. So when they started tour talk, I checked out.

Tin Garden had a reputation for overindulgence, but I was the only one in the group who'd used heavier substances. When Vail and I split up, she went to the press with that shit, and we as a band never recovered from the stigma of it. The press enjoyed reminding me of my drug usage on the daily, never letting up, and I needed to change the reputation of the other guys, who didn't use. I was entertaining thoughts about a full press statement releasing them of accusations of drug use after the album was finished. I was now cleaning up my own backyard after all my past mistakes and bad choices.

We were ready to take the *F* album to a professional studio to record it, and Rick and I were batting around the idea of where. I had every intention of leaving London to do the final album but didn't want to go to New York, where we usually went to record.

"Are we going to Jungle?" Rick asked.

"I was thinking about this castle in Ireland, not a buttoned-up studio with recording time slots. I want to have fun with this one," I replied.

"Which castle?" Rick asked.

"Kinnitty, that place where The Pogues did their live album," I replied.

"That would be cool," Rick said, tuning his guitar.

"I want to ask Red to do the 'Fucked' song," I replied.

"Red? From The Spies?" Rick asked, surprised.

"They'd be perfect," I replied.

"Back the bus up, Bas. You want to work with The Spies?" Rick said in disbelief.

"For one song," I replied with certainty.

"You know we will be drinking all night with that lot, right?" Rick said, laughing.

"That's the intention," I replied, with a straight face.

"You're serious, Bas? I thought you were on the wagon," Rick asked.

"I am, but I'm going to unhitch the horse for this album, leaving the drugs behind this time," I replied.

"What's up?" Rick asked, looking at me oddly.

"Nothing's up," I replied.

"I'll call Stan and have him book the castle for a few weeks, but should I tell him to stay home?" Rick asked, laughing.

"Yep, and call Lacey and Goth. I'll call Red," I replied.

"You're serious with this?" Rick said, looking at me in disbelief.

"We're going to Ireland, Rick ... Put your drinking boots on," I replied firmly.

I chose Kinnitty because I'd gone there on a drinking bender after my split from Vail. The castle had a tricked-out dungeon that was converted into a bar. It was popular with Irish bands that either recorded or got married in the joint. I knew that I had to get Gina hip to the idea that I would be in Ireland for a few weeks while she would have to stay home with Adonis, so I was preparing myself to deal with that. When the guys left, I headed upstairs to go to bed. Gina was coming out of Adonis's room, telling me she'd had a time getting him down for the night.

"What's up?" Gina asked me.

"My cock, for one thing," I replied with a smirk.

"Ok, so what do you want me to do about that?" Gina said with her arms folded.

"Fix the problem," I said, laughing.

"Ok, smartass, what's going on?" she replied.

"Baby, let's relax. I had a long day. Can you just get me off so I can go to sleep?" I said, as I got into bed.

"Seriously?" she said, with an attitude.

"What? Do you want me to make love to you instead?" I replied in a cool manner.

"For a moment, you must have thought I was one of your groupies," she said.

"Okay, baby, I'm sorry," I said, not wanting to tell her that I was headed to Ireland before I got off first. Gina and I made love, and then I turned over to go to sleep. But she knew that I had something on my mind and started in with the twenty-questions game.

"Something is going on, Sebastian. Spill it," Gina said.

"I'm tired, G. We'll talk tomorrow," I said, rolling over.

"You're going on tour and don't want to tell me?" Gina asked, starting in on me.

"No, G, we're recording," I replied.

"Why the secrets?" she asked.

"Fuck, G, I want to go to sleep," I replied, angered.

"You're going back to New York, aren't you?" Gina asked, nervously.

"No, G, were staying in Europe," I replied, blowing her off.

"Does that mean London?" she asked.

"Goddammit, I want to go to sleep. Fuck!" I said, really angry.

"Next time hide your 'I have something to tell you' face better," she said, with an attitude.

"Goodnight, baby," I replied, shutting this convo down.

"Goodnight, jackass," she replied. I didn't engage with her further.

Around 5:00 a.m., I got up out of bed. Gina was still sound asleep. I walked into Adonis's room and picked him up from his crib. As I held him, I started getting very emotional. I had things going through my head about Tin Garden and my future with the band. I didn't want to tour anymore, and I was struggling with one of my inner demons—drinking and being in a party frame of mind. I knew doing this album was the right decision to make for my little family, but I wanted nothing more than to be with my son. I put Adonis back down and went back to bed.

The next morning, Gina was with Adonis in his room while I was downstairs getting coffee started, contemplating how to have a conversation about Ireland, figuring that leaving a note on the way to Heathrow would be easier. She came downstairs holding Adonis.

"Hey, babe, I got coffee ready. Grab a cup and sit down," I said.

"You're ready to talk now?" Gina replied.

"Gina, sit down … please," I asked, serious.

"What's going on, Sebastian? You seem upset," she replied.

"Babe, I'm going to Ireland for a few weeks to record the new album," I replied.

"Oh, I see … Will Emily be joining Rick?" she asked, as she stood back up.

"I don't know what Rick's plans are, Gina, but I need to do this for myself, without you," I replied, looking at her as she put Adonis over her other shoulder.

"Oh … so there's girls?" she asked, turning to look at me.

"Let's talk about that. I know that you think getting sucked off is the same as intercourse. I don't see it like that. I'm never going to leave you for a fucking groupie, Gina," I replied, aggravated.

"Oh, so there will be girls? That's great," she replied.

"Chip's single, so yes, probably. And by the way, I'll be drinking," I said, as she looked at me dead in the eyes. "Gina … I'm done touring. I haven't told the guys yet, and that piece of info stays here. No inserting Leon into that. It can't get back to Em."

"What do you mean? Are you leaving Tin Garden?" she asked.

"I want to do other things in music. You know I hate touring," I replied.

"Does Rick know this?" she asked.

"No, G, but I need your support," I replied.

"You have my support, Sebastian," Gina replied. "But this is a small group with big mouths. You know where I stand on the girl issue."

"Noted, baby," I replied. I gave her a smile and finished my coffee. I told her I would take a walk on the property with Adonis while she was making breakfast. I ran into Nigel, who was planting some flowers down by the lake.

"All right then, Bas? How's the boy?" Nigel asked.

"He's good. I'm headed to Ireland, and I wanted Melba to look in on Gina while I'm away," I said as he put down the shovel.

"Ya be heading off to Eire without her then?" Nigel asked, surprised.

"Doing an album, Nigel," I stated.

"It's a shame the family won't be joining ya," Nigel said, looking down.

"I have to do this one on my own," I said.

"Running never solved a man's problems, only created new ones. The baby brought a change you weren't expecting," Nigel said, tugging on Adonis's shirt.

"You know me well, Nigel," I stated, with a smile.

"She's a good lass, and the boy is a chip off the old block, right, Bas?" Nigel asked.

"Yep," I replied, with little emotion.

"You're a lucky man. Got everything you wanted—a good wife, a son, a nice home. What else you want, then, Bas?" Nigel asked with a puzzled look on his face.

"I need to go off the reservation for a bit, sort some stuff out," I replied.

"You didn't do that before you married her, then?" Nigel asked.

"I'm doing it for them, Nigel," I said. He gave me an inquisitive look. I'd lived a selfish and one-sided life until Adonis, with no thought of the next day. I didn't want Adonis to grow up like David without his father in the house. I knew what I had to do. I had to make the best damn album before I moved into the next phase of my life.

Whiskey in the Jar

A s I got ready to leave for a few weeks, I had to admit I was looking forward to it, though with some mild hesitation. Being away
from my family was not an ideal situation for me, however going away
would make Gina and me a stronger family unit. I had to do this for
her and Adonis. I was setting us up for life.

I went outside to the home studio and placed a call to Red from
The Spies. He answered the phone and was taken off-guard hearing
my voice.

"Red, it's Sebastian Roland. It's been awhile. I have a question
for you." I had gotten along professionally with Red, but we weren't
tight. I hated their music.

"Sebastian Roland, what brings you to my blower?" Red replied.

I spent ten minutes laying out my request for The Spies to join
Tin Garden on the *F* song followed by thirty minutes of listening to
Red spin an Irish tale about his drunken night in the custody of Her
Majesty's pleasure in Belfast.

"The only thing I ask, mate, is that the song be complete shite and
we do it on the craic," Red said, agreeing to do the song on one condition: the song had to have no commercial success. The Spies were the
quintessential punk rock blokes who didn't give two fucks if anyone
listed to their music or not. The guys were full of piss and vinegar
and had a huge following with people Gina's age, the twenty-five and
under crowd, who bought everything these guys did. They were Irish
dudes who got famous for using the f-word on every song and were
known for having beer bottles rolling around on the studio floor when
they recorded. Their music was stupid, and I needed them. They were
a perfect fit for Chip's song. With The Spies on board, my financial
outlook included the Bank of England dumping cash at Mansion
Roland's doorstep.

I ended my conversation with Red. "So we will see you next week,
then?"

"The Tin Garden lot needs to be ready for a good night on the lash. The Spies don't behave like altar boys in the studio," Red replied, laughing.

"Don't want to take the piss out of you, Red, but neither do we. See you next week, then," I replied, picturing him in my head as a baby with his mom giving him a baby bottle full of Guinness instead of milk as I hung up the phone.

I headed back to the house to tell Gina what was going to happen. If she found out that we were recording with The Spies and I didn't tell her, it could end my marriage. For some ungodly reason, she loved this band.

"Gina," I yelled from the kitchen. "Gina!"

"I'm in the library with Adonis," she replied.

"I'm headed to Ireland next week ..., and before you hear it from Leon, Tin Garden is recording a song with The Spies."

"Wait, what? You're going to record with The Spies?" she asked.

"Yep," I replied.

"You hate them," she said.

"I don't hate the money they generate," I replied with a smirk.

"Since when have you ever cared about that?" she asked.

"Since I took on this house, Nigel and his family, you, and Adonis," I replied.

"You're the one who came to Greece. I didn't ask you to go there," she said.

"What does that mean, Gina?" I asked.

"What that means, Sebastian, is that I had a life in New York that I left," she said.

"So, you're saying what?" I asked, aggravated.

"I don't have a life that is my own Sebastian," she whined.

"What you have is a husband and son who love you," I stated.

"A husband who is in his studio all day and talks about getting blow jobs from groupies. I know what goes on in that head of yours," she complained.

"What does that mean, Gina?" I asked.

"I'm tired, Sebastian," she replied.

"I'm doing this for us, G," I stated.

"Sebastian, you only do things that serve you," she said sharply.

"You're never going to forgive me for the road shit, are you?" I replied flippantly.

"Wrong … I did forgive you, a long time ago. The problem is, you never forgave yourself for it." Gina paused and looked back at me. "Forgiveness starts from within, Sebastian," she said, making no sense.

"If you're pissed off about The Spies, then be pissed off about that. Don't make it about something else. God, you can be annoying," I stated, wanting her to get to the point she wanted to make.

"You pulled the plug on my career. Pardon me if I'm pissed," she replied.

"Then make your argument about that, not about other shit," I replied.

"Fine, Sebastian … I hate that I'm not singing anymore," she said, finally getting to her point.

"Ok, so now we're getting someplace. If you want to sing, do it. I never stopped you. All I ever said was *no bueno* to Tin Garden tours. I'm not going to be Paul to your Linda and teach you piano so we can do the Wings thing. Fuck no, G. But feel free to do your own thing. Fuck, I wish you would," I stated, over the back-and-forth.

"You can really be dramatic," she replied.

"And you can really be a pain in the ass. Try being a little less tactile in your thinking patterns. You really know how to take shit to another level," I stated.

"You hunted me down in Greece. You didn't have to," she said sarcastically,

"You really do piss me off," I stated, angered.

"You love the drama, Sebastian," she replied.

"Believe me, if I knew what it was about you, I would turn that shit off," I said.

"You love me; admit it," she said with a smile.

"I do … but you're not going to Ireland," I said, offering a smile back in her direction when she turned around.

Our arguments were never about the subject at hand, and it annoyed me to no end. She was the master when it came to inserting circular logic into important conversations. The beast that lived inside her brain had this built-in defense mechanism that took over her mouth. Gina was mad that she was no longer a backup singer for Tin Garden and used groupies as her weapon of choice to blame me for it. I was making big plans for our future, and she wanted to talk about minutia that required zero thought processing. When Gina was in this headspace, forget it. For the big decisions I wanted to talk about, I had to fly solo.

At 5:30 a.m., I got up and walked into Adonis room. I held him and said, "Daddy loves you." I knew it was going to be a while before I saw him again. Standing there holding him and looking out the window, I knew I was making the right decision. I put him back down in his crib and stood at the door looking at him before I left.

I got my stuff and headed to the airport. I didn't say goodbye to Gina, who was still sleeping. I had been thinking about this day for weeks. I was getting off the marriage reservation for a while, and this was my escape route. I had no intention of waking her up just to start another argument. I arrived to the airport and caught the flight to Dublin. After landing, I rented a car and headed over to Kinnitty Castle.

Walking into the castle, girls ran past me as I was putting my suitcase down. My band members were stumbling from the library bar with Red behind them. Red was holding a bottle of Jameson whiskey, shouting, "Bas hurry up mate. Girls want to do Irish car bombs."

Chip approached with two girls, one of them broke away from his arm, wanting to follow me up to my room, "you look like you could use some company," she said, as I picked my bag up from the floor.

"I'm a married man sweetheart," I said, unamused.

"That's what they all say," she replied, as she took her hand, going for my cock. She wasn't shy about it. I asked Chip to walk with me, less the groupie. I was there to work, not play around. I wanted him to get rid of the girls.

"Bas, we always have girls hanging out," Chip said, confused, "these girls have been here the last few nights. It is getting kind of old," he mumbled, frustrated.

"You think?" I replied, pointing out the fact. "Get rid of them Chip." I said, determined to get down to business.

I'd started my exit plan from Tin Garden the day tour talk started. One more crazy tour would've probably put my six feet under. Having access to substances on tour, which was preferred over everything else I had access to, I wanted to see for myself if I was capable of staying off the shit while recording, and if I was able to stay faithful to Gina long enough to finish the album.

I headed into the library bar, as Chip was scooting girls out of the castle. I saw Tiger at the bar and walked over. He and I had some unsettled business to take care of.

"Want a shot Bas?" Tiger asked, nervous.

"I want you tell tell me the truth," I demanded.

"What are you talking about?" Tiger asked, snickering taking a drink of beer.

"Gina. Did you hit that?" I asked, aggravated.

"No mate. I could have though," Tiger said with a smirk.

"You fucking asshole!" I said, as I grabbed him by the shirt and pushed him back into the bar. Rick and Red may have expected the fight was coming, they came running over, separating us, after I got a nice hook into Tiger's face.

I'd heard the Tiger and Gina rumors while we were on the "Wait Tour." I needed to get to the bottom of it, which for me was taking a few swings at Tiger. After I calmed down, we assumed the rumor was road fodder, more than likely a story concocted by Emily. I apologized to Tiger, then handed him the bottle of whiskey. We both took a swig from it, we'd buried the hatchet.

After several hours of drinking and tour bantering with the guys, we decided to head to the dungeon and start recording. Goth had the dungeon set-up for us to record the album. The dungeon was dark and moody, but also had a bar. By now everyone was hammered enough to do the "fucked" song. Shit, everyone had been drinking for the last two days before I'd even shown up to the castle. By the time we put

Red on the mic he was completely blitzed out of his mind. Beer bottles could be heard rolling around on the tracks while he was singing and it was perfect. After Red did Chip's song, I asked Goth if we needed to do another take. "No way SoBo, we captured gold," he said, as I smiled ear to ear.

After a few more hours in the dungeon, girls started to join us downstairs to party. My way of having fun on this trip was to freak everyone out with a ghost story I'd heard about, scaring the shit out of the girls so they would go into whoever's room for the night. I had a few of them convinced they were seeing a ghost, and we may have actually seen one called "Hugh." We were all kind-of drunk, and saw this shadow thing floating around, can't be one-hundred percent sure if it was Hugh or not. At 6:00 a.m. the girls freaked-out, convinced they were seeing a ghost, left with Goth. He was walking behind them, giving me a thumbs up. "I wasn't lying about that shit," I said to Goth, who ran up the stairs, scared as shit. I headed to my room and made a call to Gina, who by now was up with Adonis.

"Hey babe," I said, when Gina answered the phone.

"Just now going to bed?" Gina replied, a bit aggravated.

"Yep," I said, exhausted.

"It's early. Any girls with you?" Gina asked, inquisitively.

"There are a ton of girls here G, but not with me," I said, being honest.

"Good for you baby. Lacey is keeping me dialed in your ghost stories," She replied, happy.

"I know she is. Goodnight baby," I said, as I passed out on my pillow.

I woke up around 3:00 p.m. and headed downstairs I, the only one awake, noticed a note laying on the bar.

> "Had a great night on the lash. That ghost story you spun was complete shite, but got me laid. Cheers mate. Red. "

Just as I finished reading the note, Rick came in, "hey Bas,"

"Red and Tiger split," I said, as I handed Rick the note. Deciding if I should tell my brother the news that I was leaving the band since we were alone, but thought it better to wait until after we finished recording the album.

Two weeks had gone by fast. Word got around the campfire that the castle had been converted into, "The den of Caligula." Guys we knew in other bands, came over to hang out during our recording sessions. Other bands would sit in and jam with us. They were guys that we had toured with in the past, and they always brought girls with them. After recording all day, I'd hang out for awhile, have a few beers, spin a few ghost stories, then go to bed solo. That's how it was for me.

On August 11, I'd finished recording my last album with Tin Garden, but still needed to tell Rick I was leaving the band. Rick started in with "Greek speak," but I spoke back in English, making him converse with me in English. "Joe's coming later," Rick said, with a smirk.

"Getting rid of Lacey, Rick?" I replied.

Rick must have thought Joe could distract Lacey long enough so not to interfere with "shag fest," but when the heart and head are not attached to the dick, getting-off, is just a carnal act. I'd packed my rental car and was ready to head back to the airport. But I still had to sit the guys down. I went into the library bar where Chip and Rick were drinking and talking with Goth.

"Ready to finally have some fun?" Rick said, with a laugh.

"There is no easy way to say this…I'm leaving Tin Garden," I said, with a stern look over in Rick's direction.

Rick with the look of Toro the Bull in his eyes, came charging my way, "You fucking asshole," he yelled, taking me down to the floor. Rick was trying to get shots to my face and we were beating the shit out of each other for a good few minutes. His ass kicking from me, was long overdue.

"Fuck it, let them go for it," Chip said to Goth before they started pulling us apart.

"You knew you were leaving the day you got here," Rick said, as Goth was holding him.

My decision to exit stage left from Tin Garden, was the right one. I'd learned something in rehab, how to love myself. I was far from perfect, but, everything I had was, and they were waiting for *me* to come home.

"I'm outta here…" I said, as I left.

NBC Studios, New York, August 12, 1988.

Leon Taylor interview, already in progress.

Interviewer: What are your thoughts about Sebastian Roland leaving Tin Garden?

Leon: I thought you wanted me here today to talk about L. T.

Interviewer: Sebastian's wife Gina is the face of L. T. How did that come about?

Leon: Gina is a good friend and a New York girl who embodies what my line is all about: fashion, sass, and attitude. I asked her to do it.

Interviewer: We couldn't get Tin Garden for a comment, not even their manager. Are you surprised by the news of Sebastian leaving the band?

Leon: No, I'm not. You should've asked the cats from Raiders of Doom if you wanted a comment about Sebastian... Look, he and his family are fine. They are very happy. Let's leave it at that.

Interviewer: What will Sebastian do now?

Leon: How about this, we talk about something current. I have a clothing line that was the hit of the Paris runway. Tin Garden is yesterday's news.

Tell Me You Want Me: My Journey of Synchronicity

*T*ell Me You Want Me is a fictional rock-and-roll love story cushioned between the nonfiction world of night clubs and the music scene of the late eighties. It is inspired by the time I spent in New York. The intention was to give the reader a glimpse into the backstage world of the music industry, with a love story sprinkled in that supported nightclubs and touring. Ending *Tell Me* on cliffhanger was intentional, but it was not done to sell more books, only to let readers decide for themselves how Gina's story ended. I also wasn't sure if I would get the chance to have another book published. Sebastian's storyline was intended to end very differently than it does in this book. I made a creative—or more accurately, a responsive—decision when unexplainable events surrounding *Tell Me* started happening right after the book was released. I spent several months debating whether to open up my personal life to share this story, taking a long sabbatical from writing due to the extraordinary things that had developed as I became laser-focused on a writing project that was supposed to be just for fun.

When I worked in the world of advertising, my job could have been viewed as a stand-up comedy act where paying clients took a back seat to some pretty funny minds. Our twisted little group was in charge of some top-ranking companies' advertising dollars; if they knew that most of their campaigns were based around movie quotes, they would've been devastated.

In advertising, you draw on some of your crazier experiences as a source of inspiration. For me, that meant reliving my wild days of youth gone by, spinning wild stories for coworkers about my former, happier single life filled with drugs, nightclubs, and celebrities. I had fun when I was younger, but I had worked my ass off.

When I told animated stories to coworkers, they would say, "You need to write a book." I thought about it over the years, but I never assumed anyone outside my circle of friends and coworkers would be interested in reading about working in the catering industry for the music elite. It really wasn't that exciting. I had a short-lived career in the music industry, but I wasn't famous or a groupie with wild sex stories to write about. If I had been, I wouldn't write about them anyway. I'm not knocking those who have, of course; I think those books are fabulous. But I had an idea about how to share my past in a way that was interesting to the average reader, which would be to take some of the more vivid events I had been exposed to as inspiration and turn them into a work of fiction. That seemed more interesting, but it needed something—a love story to support it.

One afternoon, I was rehashing a tale about a guy from my husband's former band who put a garden hose through an open window and turned on the water to flood his house and piss off his soon-to-be ex-wife when they were going through their divorce, and an idea came. I began to recall crazy backstage events I had been exposed to, along with my lost youth spent in New York nightclubs, and the inspiration for *Tell Me You Want Me* was formed.

The first thing I started on was character development. The characters were not based on people that I knew. Some of the mannerisms were inspired by people I had worked with or knew of, but not the character's story lines. Writing the book in the first person as Gina was easier for me, having never written a book. The name Sebastian came about because it was a good rock-and-roll name.

One morning, I arrived at the ad agency and noticed a new guy that my company had hired. He said he was going to train me in sales. I said, "You must be kidding," and I decided on that day in July 2015 to take a three-month sabbatical to focus on my writing full time. My husband, Jim, who was surprised by this revelation, supported my decision but saw my writing endeavor more as a hobby rather than a career choice. We were having some marital issues before I took a break from the working world, and it would be easy to say that seeing something to completion, such as writing, was out of the norm for my personality. However, I had this determination. Something was driving this bus, and I went with it.

Each day while on hiatus from the working world, I could be found sitting at the kitchen table from 7:00 a.m. until around 3:00 a.m., writing out the plot of *Tell Me*, knowing how the story would end and working backward. I never left the house during those three months, other than to do short errands. I was highly focused on writing seven days a week, with some abiding help from Spotify. To say that I was attached to my little project would be an understatement. Even Jim was taken by surprise by my determination.

In early November 2015, I was getting near the end of this little writing project and noticed one afternoon that I had lost around thirty pounds. The weight loss took me by surprise, because it seemed unreasonable, given that I'd been spending massive amounts of time at a kitchen table, not doing any physical activity during those months. I hadn't noticed the weight loss before that day, and the only change in habit I can recall, was drinking a ton of Bret Michael's version of Diet Snapple, and now swear by it as a magic weight-loss program.

By the end of November, the process of publishing my first book was in full swing. I was now struggling with larger issues in my marriage, but I was happier because I'd lost weight for no apparent reason. I figured what I needed to do was to change up my look; then maybe Jim might take notice of me. I went to a hairdresser who drastically changed my hairstyle. Later that evening, sitting at the kitchen table writing, I heard the key slide into the lock on the door and perked up as Jim walked in. With a huge smile, I looked up at him. He walked by me, saying only, "Hey," and then took off for his office, which housed bass guitars. The feeling when he walked by, taking no notice of my transformation, at first left me feeling raw and in disbelief, but then that feeling quickly changed to anger. "Really? Flip you and your Fender."

A few days passed, and Jim still hadn't said anything about my new look. In fact, he took no notice of my hair being six inches longer from the extensions my hairdresser put into my hair. On the third day of him not saying anything about the new do, I asked, "Do you notice anything different about me?"

"No, why?" he said.

With that reply, I went to the bedroom, grabbed my clothes, put them in my suitcase, and headed for the front door. When he saw me with a suitcase in hand, he asked, "Where are you going?"

"I'm moving out," I said, and I left and drove over to the house of a friend who happened to be out of town for the holiday. Having keys to her place, I stayed there for a few weeks until Jim found a new place to live.

Now I admit, I had joined a dating website in November and started communicating with someone online. I was in unknown territory with the online-dating thing, with no experience in navigating it. The only thing I knew from other people who did date online was that you would either meet out for coffee or for a one-off hookup. Being a true romantic by nature, the one-night stand thing didn't work for me by default.

Around Christmas, I was in full communication online with Ben. We had been sending e-mails for a few weeks, until I finally asked him, "Is this just going to be a pen pal thing?" Ben arranged for us to meet a few days after Christmas for the typical coffee date. When I met him in the coffee shop, I noticed right away he looked totally different from his online photos. When he stood up when we were ready to leave, I saw I was taller than him. It bothered me, but I gave Ben a chance. He was pleasant and nice enough. Our conversation was normal, but strange things about my book started unfolding during the same time period. I met someone by the name of Mark Grant and overheard the name Lex Lenord being called over a PA system. I thought, *Okay, you're not losing it. What you really need is a break from everything book related.* What I needed was a distraction, and that for me was Ben.

Ben and I started our little relationship after New Year's. We took a few trips to see shows and go to sporting events. I liked Ben, but I kind of assumed after dating him that he was seeing a ton of other people. Ben dating other people didn't bother me, only him denying it. I wasn't in the space for a serious relationship, but I wanted more than a spin and toss.

In mid-March, he and I took a trip together to see a very famous band, complete with VIP passes that included a sound check, an open bar, and front row seats. On day one of this trip, I knew our "thing" was winding down. On the evening of the concert, I started ignoring Ben's attitude toward me, drinking the free cocktails heavily to drown out his negative vibe.

The following day, we were scheduled to leave in the afternoon, but a really bad storm had come through, and all the flights in and out of Phoenix were cancelled. Realizing we were stuck spending another evening together, Ben went to his social media app and saw he had some friends that were in town. He made plans for "us" to go and see them because "he" had nothing else better to do.

After our little outing, we took a cab back to our hotel. Ben got out of the car and asked me to pay the bill. My karma should have been paid forward that evening, dealing with Ben for another night. We managed to get on the last flight the following evening, and when we got back to my house, he was insistent on taking my suitcase to my door, obviously trying to get himself invited in. I didn't indulge him, though, and never saw him again. I was done with Ben, chapter closed.

A few days later, I paid a visit to my friend, a spiritual healer by trade, and told him what had happened with "the Ben." My friend had known that our thing was doomed from day one, because he was the transition guy after my failed marriage, and my friend was very happy for me to be moving on from that experience. He said to me, "Your bandwidth is narrowing; it's time to get serious." He insisted that my tolerance level for bullshit was falling.

I guess I had learned the art of setting boundaries after dating "the Ben," telling my friend that my perfect man didn't exist. My friend shook his head no and asked me to give him a detailed description of what my "perfect man" looked like. I didn't see the point in his exercise and looked at him funny. He said, "Entertain me; send me a list. I want to see what you come up with."

I went home, sat down at my computer, and pondered the question. What did he look like? As I was typing, I saw an image of a guy sitting in an airplane seat looking out the window in deep thought. I sent my friend the following e-mail on April 13, 2016:

> My perfect man would be tall with shoulder-length, dark hair and a nice build. He would be really handsome, striking, Mediterranean looking. He'd be someone who, when our eyes locked, I would know was the one. He would be nice, a bit shy, and not arrogant. He would like to travel. He'd have given up on relationships because of meeting the wrong people, much like I have. Ideally, he would have no children and would have been searching for his soul mate or twin soul, if even a thing exists, and have given up, much like I did. I would meet him traveling or in some random chance meeting. I'd want him to be the romantic type. He would also have to be a really good lover and a good conversationalist, smart and well traveled. I don't really care what he does for a living as long as it's honest. I've always imagined I would ideally be with someone who had an international job that required travel and that I would get to go on some trips with him. I want a partner—not necessarily someone to be married to but someone who just gets me.

After I sent the list to my friend, he replied, "Be careful what you ask for." I paid no attention to his comment at the time, only because I'd never seen the point in doing the exercise. Just to be clear, my friend had said to give him a list of what my perfect guy "looked like," not anything more than that. I took the exercise literally, not reading anything into this.

Later that evening, I was talking to my friend Chad on the phone and told him about the list assignment. Chad said to forget the list; what I needed was to join another dating website. And at his insistence, I did. He insisted that it would be a really good idea to get back out there and meet more people. I really didn't want to try another dating website, preferring just to stay focused on the direction I was taking in life, and started on some heavy-duty self-reflection.

During this period, I would sit in a local church a couple of days a week, not because I was religious but because it felt better sitting in a church trying to figure out what to do with my life, always wondering if higher powers ever listened. I knew the one thing that was missing: I'd always wanted to meet "the one." I knew I hadn't ever met this person and wasn't sure if such a thing even existed, but I was intrigued by the concept of a twin-flame relationship, as it is typically called.

One afternoon in church, I took a seat in one of the pews in the front row and sat there for about ten minutes looking at the cross. I then got up and left the church, and as I looked toward a cross on the roof while driving out of the parking lot, a thought came into my head: *Put him on my path.* I headed home, and as I approached a stop light, getting ready to turn onto my street, I noticed the car in front with a license plate that read ANGEL. I grabbed my phone and took a photo of the coincidental sighting after leaving a spiritual place.

After I got home, I headed outside to my patio with my phone and started checking my online dating messages from the new site Chad had insisted I join. I had a few waiting and started going through them. I noticed one waiting from someone I will call "Ray." He was a really cute guy I had seen earlier on the site and added to my list.

I was checking out Ray's photo when I paused from typing a response back to him, I looked up at the sky and noticed a rainbow, being memorized by seeing one with no rain. "So, is he the one?" I said, laughing because of the angel license plate from earlier. I continued replying back to Ray's message.

Ray e-mailed me back right away and seemed interested in meeting. We had a conversation going for a bit. He mentioned what he did for a living and that he enjoyed travel, making a point of adding that he knew some Greek, probably because I had mentioned that Greece was my favorite place to vacation. Ray mentioned that he was out of town at the moment, but we made a very loose plan to meet for coffee later in the week.

A few days later, I heard a ping on my cell phone. Ray had messaged me that he was back in town and that we could meet near my house. It was a welcome change from the standard "hey, want to get together later" messages coming in at 10:00 p.m. Ray was one of the nice ones. After reading his message, I walked across the street to the store. As I crossed the intersection, I started noticing dimes laying in the street in a pattern, but I didn't bother to pick up the strange trail of coins that seemed to form a sort of yellow brick road to the market. At the door of the store, I looked down, and a dime and three pennies caught my attention. Again, I just left them.

I walked back from the store and was digging for keys in my purse at the front door when I heard something hit the patio table. I looked over and saw it was a dime. I was startled, since it had come out of nowhere, and I turned around to see who the dime fairy was. It freaked me out, especially since I had seen all those dimes earlier.

Later that same afternoon, Ray sent me a message that he had found a Greek document. "Thought of you; what a coincidence." I thought, *Coincidence? No, you're trying to be cute.* We then firmed up plans to meet the next day.

The following day, I arrived for our coffee clutch, looking at Ray's profile photo so I could find him. I started getting nervous because of my previous experience with Ben. Ray spotted me and approached. I thought at the time that he actually looked better in person, and unlike Ben, he had not added an extra four inches to his height description. We got in line for coffee. Standing there talking with him, it seemed as if I knew him from someplace. I assumed I would figure out where after we took a seat and started talking, but I never did.

A few minutes into our conversation, he told me that he was married but separated and other things that you normally wouldn't share with someone within the first few minutes of meeting, but I appreciated his honesty and was in the same kind of situation as he was. I felt very comfortable talking with him, as our conversation seemed to flow easy, but it did feel rushed. I couldn't tell if he liked me or if he was just being polite. Ray was not the easiest person to read. The meeting lasted an hour. We exchanged numbers and then went our separate ways.

That Monday, as I sat at work, Ray sent a message to see how I was doing. We made plans for Friday after work. That morning my e-book stubs of *Tell Me* had come in the mail from the publisher, and I'd put a few in my purse before heading to work. I meet Ray later at a bar located down the street from the office where I worked. He noticed me sitting inside, came in, and sat down. We proceeded to order drinks and have a great conversation. Talking with him, it felt to me like I had known him a really long time. It was kind of crazy to hit it off with someone that well. We started looking into each other's eyes, and it got really intense.

"I really like you," he said. Then he wanted to know what I was thinking after he said it. He just sat there and smiled, never taking his eyes off of me.

The phrase *Where have you been my entire life?* didn't come out. The biggest regret one can have is not having the courage to say what is in one's heart and head. I turned away, too shy to answer his question

Our conversation continued to flow the entire evening. We talked about music and travel. When Ray asked me about being a writer, I reached into my handbag, pulling out one of the *Tell Me* book stubs and handing it to him, never expecting him to read it. We continued to talk in the bar for a few more hours. We got each other's silly senses of humor and took a few selfies earlier in the evening. I knew Ray liked me; he had already expressed it verbally. He planted a pretty romantic kiss on me after we had just been acting silly. By now it was getting late, and more patrons were starting to arrive at the bar, making it difficult to hear one another. So, we decided to leave. Ray walked me to my car, which was located near Sixth Street. (The significance of this will be disclosed later.) He kissed me goodnight, but he pulled back from me when it got heated and made no plans to see me again. He did send me a very short, sweet text message after I got home, though.

A few days after our date, my friend Chad, a very to-the-point, no-bullshit airline pilot, was in town on an overnight from work. My hardbound books of *Tell Me* had just been delivered when Chad came in the door. I didn't give him time to settle in; I was excited to tell him all about the date with Ray, babbling on about how we seemed to have hit it off and thanking Chad for the suggestion to join the dating site. I grabbed my phone to show Chad the photo we took at the bar, along with Ray's picture from the dating site. A very odd expression came splashing across his face as he looked at Ray's photo and the books sitting on my table. Chad picked up one of the books and said, "Are you kidding me? Look at this."

Taking my phone and enlarging Ray's profile photo to show only the bottom part of his face, Chad laid the phone on top of the book next to the depiction of Sebastian on the *Tell Me* cover. We couldn't believe what we were looking at; it was the same person. Chad said, "You didn't show Ray this, did you?"

I told Chad that I'd given Ray one of the book stubs but hadn't noticed the similarity until just then.

"Jesus, you manifested this dude," Chad said, laughing and shaking his head at me as he walked away into the other room, yelling back, "You may have just messed up your chances. That is too weird." He left me staring at this odd coincidence in disbelief.

The *Tell Me* cover had been designed by Lane Bullard several months before I met Ray. Lane was briefed about the story's contents and designed two options for me to choose from. When I saw the option that we ended up selecting, I said to her, "That's him. That's Sebastian."

A few days went by, and I got a text from Ray asking me how my day was going. We made another plan to meet for a drink. This time, it was an afternoon outing on a Wednesday. He selected the location, and I would meet him after work. As we sat at the bar, I noticed that the intensity of the eye contact we'd shared the previous week seemed to have faded. He seemed very distant or preoccupied. He mentioned that he was having some major family issues and would be going out of town. Then he cut our meeting short after a few hours, leaving me very confused about whether he was interested in seeing me again. When he pulled out his credit card, I happened to see that he had the book stub I had given him in his wallet. I wondered if he had been showing it to his friends to get their thoughts about whether he looked like the dude on the cover of my book. Chad was right, my chances with Ray were over due to a stupid coincidence. I was deflated, seeing it in his wallet.

When Ray walked me to my car, I knew it would be a really long time before I saw him again, if I ever did. After we hugged, I recalled something he had said to me on our second date: "When I'm done, I never look back." I felt an emptiness inside watching him walk away. He never turned around. Most people in my situation would never have spoken to the guy again. It may sound odd, but I had compassion for him. I knew his distance toward me had very little to do with that book stub.

During the next few months, Ray had major things he was dealing with. I kept in contact via text messages to touch base. Call me the nice girl who finishes last. I can't seem to play the role of mean girl, but I could use some attitude adjustment to accommodate the thrill of the chase. Now, I'll admit fully that I was the one who was initiating all of our contact during this time, but he always replied, never giving me any reason to think I shouldn't see how he was doing. Our text conversations would continue randomly over the next several months, but we never saw each other during this time period.

One afternoon in July 2016 as I got ready to leave work, a thought of Ray entered my mind. I wondered how he was doing and thought, *May you be watched over and protected.* I left my office and walked to my car. As I passed by the hood, I saw there was a dime sitting on it. The sun was reflecting off of it, catching my attention. I saw the dime and thought, *What is it with the dimes?* Picking it up and putting it in in my pocket, I got into my car and started the drive home.

The events that I'm about to describe, Ray was only recently made aware of. They are what had me debating whether to open up and share this story at all. I'll admit I'm embarrassed, as it all sounds crazy, but the events did happen, and there is no logical explanation for what I'm sharing.

As I headed home from work, I turned on the radio in an area with really bad cell phone and radio reception. The station I was listening to switched over on its own to a station about three hundred miles away, and a song started: "Photograph" by Ed Sheeran. I'd never heard the song before. The lyric said, "Wait for me to come home." I didn't think it was odd that the radio had picked up a signal from another radio market; the area reception's sucked. When the song got to the very last verse about kissing under a lamppost on Sixth Street, I paused and said, "What?" The randomness of the lyrics of the song coinciding with the thought I'd had about Ray earlier took me by surprise. Hearing that last line, something clicked, and I tried to remember if that was the street where Ray had walked me to my car the night we'd had our intense-stare-down date. This song had my attention when the station went back on its own again. I paused, confused, and said out loud, "If the next song is (Ray's favorite band), then he's the one." The song that was playing was about to end, and the very next song that started was by Ray's favorite band. I was a bit taken aback but not in shock that, having called out a band by name, the radio then played that group as if on demand. I waited at a stoplight, very confused, thinking, *What's going on?*

Right at that moment, I heard something hit the passenger side window inside my car, causing me to jump. I looked down and saw that at my leg was a medallion. I picked it up, surveying it. On the side facing me were the words *trust in Jesus*. The medallion had come out of nowhere and scared the hell (heaven) out of me. I looked around inside my car and saw that the windows were up and the air was on. I was startled and pulled my car over into a parking lot. To say that I was questioning my sanity would be an understatement. That event was a full-court press from the Universe, together with the highly coincidental signs that afternoon. Being shaken, I made a call to my enlightened spiritual friend to tell him what I had just experienced. My friend, who was intrigued during the rehashing of the event, said to meet him, so I headed over to his office.

I pulled into the parking lot of my friend's business practice and walked in with rattled nerves. He was sitting in his chair, calm, cool, and collected, looking at me with a raised eyebrow.

He laughed. "The Universe is talking. Are you listening?"

He seemed more interested in asking me questions about picking up a radio signal from three hundred miles away than dealing with a message from the Messiah. I thought in the back of my mind, *I just want to know what's up with the Jesus bomb going off in my car. What is it supposed to mean?* My friend was pointing out all of the synchronicities at play between Ray and me but was reluctant to say anything about what I had just experienced with the religious message. He insisted that Ray and I had plenty of unfinished business and said that the next step would reveal itself at the right moment. Most importantly, I needed to trust myself to know when that time was.

My friend's attitude toward my experience was extremely casual, and it took me by surprise when I showed him the medallion. "Look at this thing," I said in a panic.

"And?" my friend replied.

"What do you mean, 'And?' I don't have anything like this," I said.

"And ... now you do," he replied casually with a smile.

I admitted earlier that I've never considered myself to be spiritualty enlightened and never staked a claim to any knowledge about the angelic realm, but I can assure you, I was getting fast-tracked to becoming well versed in the subject matter by external forces that had me seeking out spiritual teachers to figure this out. It appeared the Universe was bombarding me with signs to look at Ray for some reason. I had been told by people in the spiritual community that Ray and I possibly had something to heal in this lifetime. I couldn't be sold on the past-life thing, but I started looking at the words *trust* and *heal* in the overall context of the messages from the signs and the spiritual community I looked to for answers.

The following day as I opened the door to my car to head to work, I saw a dime sitting in the driver's seat. Picking it up and tossing it in the change holder, I started my car, turning on the radio. The station decided that it would like to entertain me with Ed's "Photograph" song again, at which point there was a ping on my cell phone. It was a text from Ray telling me he was back in town, which I read just as Ed was singing "wait for me to come home." Laughing out loud, I said, "Really?" Ray's message was about getting together at the end of the week. I laughed, thinking about the timing of the song and the text from Ray with the same context about being home, as I eagerly texted him back. I was really looking forward to seeing him again; it had been a few months. We made plans for him to come to my house for dinner that Sunday.

The evening before our dinner date, a strange feeling started to come over me. As I shopped for the food I was going to prepare, I thought, *I don't know why I'm doing this.* That feeling was confirmed that Sunday morning at 8:30 a.m. by a text message. Ray told me he had to go back out of town to deal with family issues again. I was disappointed that he'd sent a text; he should've called to cancel. But instinctively, I'd already known that date wasn't going to happen.

Toward the end of July, Chad came back into town for a visit and we decided at midnight that it would be a fabulous idea to drive to Las Vegas for a night. It was not one of the better decisions we've ever made, however we did the five-hour journey by car, getting caught up along the way. Chad and I had traveled the world together with our former spouses in happier times, and we were both in the same place in life, moving on from our failed marriages, though his divorce was finalized while I was still in the separation stage. Chad and I had become good friends, navigating the single world together, and our lives seemed to be tracking one another's.

We arrived in Vegas in the early morning hours and hit the casino. A few hours passed. Feeling exhausted from the drive, we left the casino floor and went up to the room to get some sleep. Around noon, Chad woke up, and we started talking. Our conversation drifted to online dating stories, and Chad decided that he would take this opportunity to lecture me about putting eggs in baskets, which really consisted of him asking how many "Ray eggs" were in my basket. Chad took a combative stance when he asked if I had ever gone back out with Ray after he flaked on our date. When I said "no," Chad started giving me his take on all things Ray, saying he was a player who had found someone else to play with. I was caught off guard, being attacked about my dating life after waking up from a long-ass drive and a short-ass nap, but I stood up for Ray. Something Chad had said in his declaration about him felt inappropriate and actually caused me to pause. I lay on my bed, looking over at Chad on his, and said, "He can't be with me because of his wife."

Upon making that declaration, the power went out in our room. Chad, with a startled look in my direction, said, "I'm going downstairs. This shit with him … freaks me out." He jumped from his bed and headed back to the casino floor.

About ten minutes later, Chad called me from his cell phone. "Get down here now! The electricity is out in the whole casino. You messed something up with this Universe crap." I got up and took the stairs, because the elevators were down from the power outage. I found Chad and saw that he was right; all of the power was out in the casino, even for the slot machines, which are usually powered by backup generators for situations like that.

Chad stood surrounded by several pissed-off slot junkies sitting at machines, waiting in the hot casino so that they could get their money back. Chad was looking around in disbelief. Then he started giving me an odd look like I had something to do with it. Playing along with this suggestion, I said, "I told you he was a nice guy," joking like I had control over the power going out. Then the music in the casino came back on, the lights flickered in the ceiling above us, and the machines came back to life. This was met with thunderous applause that echoed throughout the casino floor from the people who had to get their gambling fix going again. Chad paused and shook his head at me. He raised his hand and started to speak but then said, "Fuck it," and walked away. He said nothing more about the power thing, nor did he bring up Ray's name again on that trip. We did address the incident about a month later. Did Chad think it was a coincidence? No, not where Ray was concerned.

I reached out to Ray on that Vegas trip to see how he was doing with his overwhelming situation, only because divine forces seemed to be pushing me to check in with him. But Ray just replied with a smile emoji, leaving me totally confused about the electrical outage that had happened the moment I'd defended him to my friend. I felt

stupid contacting him, because there seemed to be no meaning behind the event. Maybe the spiritual world wanted to impart wisdom
to Chad that Ray was a nice guy. I don't know. That incident never
made any sense to me, but I always knew deep inside that it wasn't a
mere coincidence.

I tried to explain to Chad, an airline pilot by profession, that
synchronicities exist, but he never would've bought into it in a million years. He's a pilot with a checklist; everything needs to be black
and white. Relationships are either yes or no, and a guy who doesn't
initiate contact with you is a player who likes to play around. After
the Vegas incident, though, Chad, the rational, conservative pilot,
came over to the other side, changing his tune when Ray texted me
the smile emoji. Chad said, "Okay, he seems like a nice guy, but you'll
fuck it up." Thanks, Chad. Really … thanks friend.

Ray didn't reach out on his own after Vegasgate, so I stopped initiating all communication with Ray in August and moved on. Sure,
I was highly disappointed, because I thought Ray was a great guy
that liked me. He just had a lot of crap he was dealing with. Seems
Chad was sitting in the "see, what did I tell you" seat, which really
bummed me out.

By the middle of September, over a month since I had last com-
municated with Ray, we were nothing more than estranged pen pals. I
traveled back home and called on my friend Sue to see if she wanted to
meet up for coffee and get caught up on everything that had happened
since the Chicago trip we had taken together in May. I brought up
what had been going on the last several months with the signs, giving
Sue the CliffsNotes version of meeting Ray and the crazy coincidences
that followed. She froze with a startled look on her face when I told
about the incident in my car. Sue was intrigued and wanted to see
Ray's photo; she was curious about the man Jesus had chimed in on.
I picked up my cell phone, noticing the time was 4:44 p.m., and went
searching through my photos for the selfie Ray and I had taken at the
bar. When I found the photo, Sue took my phone and looked at it,
stretching the image.

"Hey, did you see this time stamp on your photo and this heart thing above your heads?" I took my cell phone back from her and could make out the heart-shaped orb thing in the photo, but I was more intrigued by the time stamp of 4:44 p.m., since I had just seen it when I'd picked up my phone. I had never noticed the time stamp before, figuring it meant nothing, just like the dimes and songs.

Sue was perplexed and thought my story was odd. She suggested that I ask a priest about the rainbow and the angel license plate. I opted out of that. I mean, I had already been on a spiritual tear through my hometown and had given up trying to sort out the meaning of these signs by now. Besides, a priest wouldn't want to hear my sordid stories about a married guy I met through a dating site and had seen only on a few occasions. Ray had ghosted me. Why bother?

Sue and I wrapped up our day, and I thought, *I need to look at that number when I get back to the house* People in the spiritual community had told me a little about numerology, but to be honest, I wasn't into it. I knew better than to go on this number-sequence hunt, but when I walked through the door, I grabbed my laptop and looked up the meaning of 444. I found out that the energy surrounding 444 is all about protection or being protected. I thought, *Okay, that's nice. Is that it?*

I had noticed random number sequences right around the time I met Ray but had never looked into their meaning. I'd never had a reason to, not until Jesusgate. I recalled the appearance of dimes before he would communicate and remembered bringing up these number sequences to my spiritual friend the day the of the medallion incident, suggesting it was one of those "it happens with him" things. The number sequences always seemed to be centered around the numbers 1111—that being a manifestation number and the doorway into synchronicities—and 444. I'll let readers decide for themselves where they stand on this. I have respect for people's beliefs. I personally didn't buy into numerology until I saw that the patterns were more than coincidence. I believe that the Universe does communicate to us using math and numbers if we are open to the communication. I know my medallion experience is odd and can't be explained, however I've never held the belief that divine powers were speaking to me.

The following morning, I persuaded my mom to meet me for breakfast at the local Waffle House, a unique dining establishment that she loathed because of the colorful clientele. When the waitress brought the check afterward, I glanced over at the amount: $11.11. I rolled my eyes and started to chuckle, because that was the first number sequence I'd noticed. Then as I approached the car, I saw a dime on the hood. I laughed, put it in my pocket, looked up at the sky, and asked out loud, "And would you care to elaborate on that?" My mom asked me what I had said, and I replied flippantly, "Never mind."

We headed over to my uncle's house to spend the day with him. When we had been there for a while, someone asked what time it was. I grabbed my phone; it was 4:44 p.m. I also noticed there was a text message waiting. I was startled when I found the name Ray staring back at me. I briskly got up and went into the bathroom with my phone. Ray had been out of contact for over a month. As I read his message, the smile that had been plastered across my face turned upside down. His short text message merely asked what time I was getting home from work. That was it. After four months, that was all he had to ask. I replied, "I'm out of town," letting him know that I would touch base with him when I returned. I assumed he was playing it safe with his communication, maybe to see if I still had interest in him or to see how I would respond to his very brief question. I was happy to hear from him but disappointed in the general context of his very short and to-the-point message.

All the signs that had been pointing me in Ray's direction always left me highly disappointed; none of the signs surrounding him ever made sense. Nothing ever seemed to connect at any given time. I wondered now if his explanations for going away were flat excuses to keep me on a back burner for when he hit a dry spell in his dating life.

The following week, I texted Ray that I was back in town, but he made no plans to see me. I had met someone that I was dating casually, but I still felt this connection to Ray that seemed "logically irrational." It was not just because of the stupid signs that couldn't be explained by simple logic; these feelings had developed before the signs with him ever started. They had arisen on our second date.

The following day, Ray texted the same question as before: what time are you getting home from work? I agreed to see him only because I was curious how he was doing. Ray stopped by, and our conversation was easy. We picked up where we had left off months prior. After a few hours of getting caught up, he asked how my book was doing and asked for a copy of it. Sitting next to him, I handed him the book, and he made his move. I had assumed correctly that Ray's text could be construed as a hookup call, and he was taken by surprise when I backed out of a good time. I wanted him, sure—he is one sexy dude—but not at the cost of being someone that he tossed after he got what he wanted. We ended up going to dinner instead.

Later in the week, Ray came over to my house and was acting silly. It didn't bother me. I was happy that he was comfortable enough around me to be like that. I loved his sweet spirit. Our conversations together were always effortless, but when he decided to tell me he had anxiety issues, he get up and said, "I know there is a reason we met. We both like each other, but we need to take things slow."

After Ray told me about the anxiety, I reflected on the time when I was writing Sebastian's storyline. I'd never clearly seen Sebastian's face in my mind, but I could see his physical outline and the way he carried himself. There was another overlooked similarity, Sebastian's storyline was written for him to speak Greek. Ray had told me about knowing the Greek language before I met him. But the aha moment came when I remembered Sebastian suffered with anxiety issues. Looking at Ray after he said that, I knew then that I was involved in some manifested synchronicity situation.

It appeared that I was hosting the real-life Sebastian right off the pages of *Tell Me* in my living room. But then I thought back to the ideal-guy list that I'd given my spiritual friend; I'd failed to mention that I wanted my dreamy guy to be single and free of complex issues. Sebastian and Ray were the same in that respect. I never expected that the antagonist from my book would be sitting in my living room. Obviously, there is no scientific proof to my story, however I do believe I channeled Ray in some way when I was writing. Perhaps quantum physics might explain a lot of the odd things that happened, like the medallion in my car and the dimes. But the number patterns and power outages that seemed to center around Ray, those would be considered synchronicity.

Sebastian and Ray both had unique, linear storylines; their physical appearances are right on, and their mannerisms and personality traits are eerily similar. That leaves one to ask the age-old question, does art imitate life, or does life imitate art? These experiences could be written off as a series of coincidences, but I believe everything in life has a meaning. The spiritual message that I received in my car had me baffled for months. I came to the conclusion later that it had nothing to do with religion; rather, it was a message for me to trust. I believe that the medallion in my car had something to do with quantum physics. Something (not someone) wanted my attention that day. Finding dimes placed on my car, hitting my patio, and laying in the street—these inexplicable events were telling me to look at Ray. The number sequences that centered around him were consistent, and I would categorize them as synchronistic events (meaningful coincidences).

Ray mentioned recently that he'd started reading *Tell Me*. He texted me, "It's intriguing." I thought, *It should be, Ray … Keep going. You'll find your twin around chapter four.* He has said to me on several occasions, "There was a reason we met." I have my own theory as to the reason; I believe him to be a mixture of two things: a meaningful coincidence and a twin soul.

The energy of twin souls is special. We're accelerating, and more people are meeting their twin connections. Typically, when meeting, there are synchronicities before, during, and after you meet. Twins are mirror versions of ourselves who show us how to be better versions of ourselves. Time is not lost when separated, as twins can talk about anything openly, probably because the twin souls share the same energetic vibration. The twin-soul connection is a very intense encounter. Well, this all sounds good, right? Wrong. There needs to be acknowledgement by both of the connection, and that's tricky, because regardless of the signs pointing to this theory—which is not really based in science but rather in Greek mythology—Ray would have to acknowledge me as his twin to make it so. Otherwise he isn't. To be very clear, just because the Universe dropped him into my in-box on a dating website, that doesn't mean Ray sees me as his twin. It doesn't work that way; free will is at play.

Twin relationships are not to be confused with soul-mate relationships. The latter are based more in the love and lust only department. Twin relationships hold some deeper meaning than that of soul-mate relationships. Twin-soul encounters are rare, and the relationship between the twins has more to do with developing our creativity, learning, growing, and healing for the soul's journey. Twin connections help us to become better versions of ourselves.

Synchronicities are meaningful coincidences that move together in time and happen when a thought occurs in the mind and is then mirrored by an external event that has no causal connection. There can be no doubt that writing my story and then finding Ray in my path was a synchronicity. Coincidences by design are to help with decision making, relationships, and spiritual development. Synchronicities hold significance but only to the person experiencing them, and they can only occur when you are open to receive the message. We all have, at some point in our lives, experienced synchronicity.

Ray will process our reason for meeting at his own pace, if he chooses to process it at all, and work out things in his life that are complicated and have nothing to do with me, or my manifestation of him, as it were. Pushing him to see any connection we share simply won't make it happen. He knows there was a reason that something brought us together.

Where are Ray and I today? As it stands, we're not lovers, and we're not friends, not in the definition of what friends really are. We currently have a business arrangement. Ray has taken on a mission to help me, or possibly himself, with a major project in my life. Outside of the monetary incentive to do so, he may have felt compelled in some way to help me. This attitude can be viewed more logically as a self-interest on his part, but that wouldn't change the dynamics of our twin-soul experience. There are some pitfalls in having a twin connection. When you meet your mirrored soul, it's usually at the most challenging time in your life. One of the twin's will be unavailable in some way, whether that means being emotionally unavailable or being involved in another relationship. While one twin chases the other runs. There is always a runner and a chaser. Guess who the chaser is? Me. Not all twin relationships are romantic. Most of them can be and some usually are, but the running twin usually leaves due to the magnetic energy. This energy is so intense in the beginning that it creates confusion, stopping any of the romantic feelings. The energy when twin souls collide is supposed to be pretty amazing, but I can't speak to that with any certain authority. It got very close, and I can say for certain that yes, the vibration was intense. I could've had a nice science report to turn in on this subject. Now knowing what I know now about this type of connection, I should've in the name of science.

Manifestations at their most basic are thoughts; be they positive or negative, like attracts like. Focus on something long enough, and it shall come to pass. I was laser-focused on my characters and thought about meeting my twin soul at the same time. I put all that energy into my writing, therefore opening the door for the synchronicities to occur.

Ray is the quintessential definition of what synchronicity is; it was all but inevitable that we would meet. I asked for him to be put him in my path. Chad suggested the path for me to travel—the dating site. On the list that my spiritual friend had me create, I'd asked for a random chance meeting and many other things. Synchronicity delivered exactly what I asked for.

What did the all of signs mean? I'm left having no idea other than what I have explained. The cover freaked Ray out at first, and who can blame him? If I could change anything about this journey, I would never have chosen the cover I did due to the drama, but if I hadn't, I may never have met Ray at all. The number of synchronicities I told him about did play a negative role, but that really has more to do with Ray than anything else. Ray probably thinks I practice magic or something. He has called me a succubus, in jest. But don't practice anything but being centered.

Where is Ray today? He's good. He has moved on from the

book-synchronicity experience. Ray had an important role on my journey in life by default. He unknowingly opened my mind to see the world differently. I can only trust that I have given back to him what he has given me. A spiritual path to walk. He is a man who is complex but kind. I have seen his sensitive side; he lets it come out sometimes. More importantly, Ray is the most wonderful meaningful coincidence I could have encountered. I'm grateful to have met him. He is one of a kind—well …He may have a doppelgänger somewhere out there.

As far as Sebastian goes, he and Gina are in some alternate universe, gone from my life experience, but they are together … till the other side of time.

About the Author

Kris Embrey is a music aficionado who worked for Dick Clark as a runner for his music production company and for several television productions that included the American Music Awards and the Academy Awards. To learn more about her, visit tellmeyouwantme. com. *Till the Other Side of Time* is her second book.

Printed in Great Britain
by Amazon